Lesley Castle

Lesley Castle

Jane Austen

ET REMOTISSIMA PROPE

Hesperus Classics

Hesperus Classics
Published by Hesperus Press Limited
4 Rickett Street, London sw6 1ru
www.hesperuspress.com

First published by Hesperus Press Limited, 2005
Reprinted 2005
Foreword © Zoë Heller, 2005

Designed and typeset by Fraser Muggeridge
Printed in Jordan by Jordan National Press

isbn: 1-84391-115-9

CONTENTS

FOREWORD

The smallness of Jane Austen's fictional canvas is probably the best-known characteristic of her mature work; even those who have never read her six great novels have heard about her 'little bit (two inches wide) of ivory'. But as a teenager, Austen had yet to establish her distinctive boundaries. She was still experimenting. One of the pleasures that this volume affords us is a glimpse of a famously 'quiet' and domestic writer engaging with melodramatic incident, regal vice and other immoral behaviour in a gleefully direct way.

'Lesley Castle', a rambunctious parody of the epistolary novel, written when Austen was sixteen, is particularly striking in this respect. On its first page, we find Margaret Lesley lamenting the dissipated ways of her fifty-seven-year-old roué father and the adulterous elopement of her sister-in-law. A death in a horse-riding accident, a couple of conversions to Roman Catholicism, and various cynical second marriages will shortly ensue. These outsized events are matched by a comic tone markedly broader and less naturalistic than anything to be found in Austen's later work. The satire keeps lapsing into burlesque. A running joke about the speciousness of the affection that the conceited female correspondents protest for one another is sent extravagantly over the top when Margaret Lesley cooingly informs Charlotte Lutterell, 'How often have I wished that I possessed as little personal beauty as you do; that my figure were as inelegant; my face as unlovely; and my appearance as unpleasing as yours!' There are even moments of physical humour – as when Lady Lesley envisages herself being hoisted up the cliff to Castle Lesley on a rope. A character called Lady Kickabout seems to have strayed out of a play by Congreve. In fact, all the protagonists have something of the cheerful excess of Restoration comedy about them. Charlotte, with her culinary monomania – her insistence on the loss of victuals being of greater import than the loss of a fiancé – is quite surreal in her dottiness. Twenty-five years later, Austen would take Charlotte's eccentricity and loquaciousness and innocence, and transmute these qualities into the comic pathos of Miss Bates; here, she is content to give us a kind of pantomime spinster.

Margaret Lesley, the novel's chief proponent of sensibility, is just as ludicrous as Charlotte in her way. But whereas Charlotte is a likeable idiot – her passion for roast beef has at least the merit of constancy – Margaret is purely awful. She is one of a long line of Austenian sillies whose romantic pretensions and delusions float, like not very effective veils, over the prosaic unpleasantness of their true natures. She fancies herself 'secluded from mankind' while, in fact, enjoying a rather busy social life in a suburb of Perth. She peppers her letters with exclamation marks to advertise her feeling heart, but swiftly proves herself utterly insensitive. She boasts of being innocent of her own charms and is, of course, pathologically conceited.

Camilla Stanley in 'Catharine' is another one of Margaret's breed. And so, too, is the flibbertigibbet narrator of 'The History of England'. Overflowing with hyperbolic opinion, but devoid of 'taste and information', neither of them has anything to teach us but the lineaments of her own prejudice. Just as Camilla can summarily dismiss the entire Dudley clan on the basis of Miss Dudley's poor taste in headdress, so the sentimental historian can point confidently to Anne Boleyn's personal loveliness as proof of her innocence.

Some commentators, puzzled by Austen's decision to endow her foolish narrator with her own pro-Stuart inclinations, have suggested that the young author is confused about tone. But fools don't always hold the wrong opinions; they are just as likely to hold the right opinions for the wrong reasons. I take it as a sign of Austen's precocious sophistication that she is willing to make light of her own allegiances by having an idiot defend them. The narrator's lines on Austen's heroine, Mary Queen of Scots – 'this bewitching Princess, whose only friend was then the Duke of Norfolk – and whose only ones now Mr Whitaker, Mrs Lefroy, Mrs Knight and myself' – are some of the funniest in the piece.

'The History of England' is a jolly, ludic work, designed to elicit laughter when read aloud in the Austen family's parlour. But there is something vaguely unsettling about the nonchalant way that the narrator proceeds through her catalogue of murder and betrayal as if she were discoursing on bonnets. A few of her more insouciant asides – 'Lord Cobham was burnt alive, but I forget what for' – have a positively Swiftian sting. As always in Austen's work, recklessness with facts and inattention to detail are the rhetorical clues to a deeper-seated, moral carelessness. Think of Lady Lesley blithely forgetting the 'long rigmarole story' she is told about the parentage of two-year-old Louisa – and with it the rather crucial fact that she is the child's grandmother. Think of the caddish Mr Stanley's repeated failure to listen when Catharine speaks. Or think of the way Camilla Stanley declares Mrs Smith's novels 'the sweetest things in the world' and, in the next breath, blithely confesses to having skipped great chunks of them. Today, these characters might be thought of as suffering from Attention Deficit Disorder. Austen's less forgiving diagnosis is rampant egotism.

In 'The History' and in 'Lesley Castle', the author's commentary is only implied. Austen's ghostly, ironic presence hovers over the text like the Cheshire Cat's smile. In 'Catharine', the most ambitious of the pieces in this volume, we get a real heroine – a protagonist, that is, in whom some of Austen's own values and intelligence are made manifest. And what fun it is to read Catharine Percival's wry rejoinders to Camilla Stanley's gush! They go unnoticed by Camilla, of course, but no matter. For Catharine, as for so many Austenian heroines, ironic wit is its own reward – a small but delicious consolation for all the indignities and constraints she is forced to suffer with quiet forbearance.

Catharine's judgement is not entirely trustworthy, of course. She is not yet a 'deep reader', and her innate kindness and decency have still to be honed by experience. The moral question that Austen sets for her is not dissimilar to that she will pose for Elinor and Marianne in *Sense and Sensibility*. What is the appropriate latitude to give to emotion? The novel's official response is clear enough: the conservative values of propriety and reserve must take precedence over romantic self-indulgence. But, as in *Sense and Sensibility*, this official response has its tensions and ambiguities. We notice, for example, that in Mrs Percival, Austen has chosen a most unattractive spokeswoman for the virtues of caution and modesty. She's a neurotic crab apple. Who can blame Catharine for chafing under her restraints? It is, of course, *absolutely* wrong for Catharine to take off for the Dudleys' ball alone with a stranger. But the flirtatious conversation between Stanley and Catharine is much the liveliest, sexiest dialogue yet seen in the story, and we, too, are a little seduced by it. We are instructed to disapprove when Catharine ignores etiquette and agrees to lead a dance with Stanley, but we are also invited to detest the snobbery of Camilla's outraged reaction.

It's not that Austen has a secret, subversive agenda. She really *does* want us to accept that a tradesman's daughter ought not to lead a dance when ladies of more noble birth are present. It's just that her instincts as a writer, as an observer of lived experience, are keener than her ambitions as a moralist. Even at the age of sixteen, she is incapable of anything diagrammatic.

At some point in the course of reading these works, you are likely to feel the prickings of a baffled envy. Even as you are absorbing the rhythms of Austen's shapely sentences, the pitch-perfect comedy of her dialogue, the sly elegance of her irony, you will stop and ask, 'How did a teenager do this?'; 'How did she know so much about the particularities and universalities of human folly?'; 'Where did she acquire such a wise and confident wit?'.

'One of those fairies who perch upon cradles must have taken her a flight through the world directly she was born,' was Virginia Woolf's suggestion (Virginia Woolf, *The Common Reader: Volume 1*, Vintage, 2003). This may seem a rather twee and unsatisfactory answer. But then, I don't think Woolf meant to offer an explanation so much as to frankly acknowledge a conundrum. Austen, it is safe to say, was some species of genius. To speak of voyages with fairies is just another way of reminding us that the mystery of that genius was, and is, irreducible.

– *Zoë Heller, 2005*

Lesley Castle

To Henry Thomas Austen Esq.[1]

Sir,
I am now availing myself of the liberty you have frequently
honoured me with of dedicating one of my novels to you. That it
is unfinished, I grieve; yet fear that from me, it will always
remain so; that as far as it is carried, it should be so trifling
and so unworthy of you, is another concern to
your obliged humble servant,
the author

Lesley Castle
3rd January 1792

My brother has just left us. 'Matilda,' said he at parting, 'you and Margaret will, I am certain, take all the care of my dear little one that she might have received from an indulgent and affectionate and amiable mother.' Tears rolled down his cheeks as he spoke these words – the remembrance of her who had so wantonly disgraced the maternal character and so openly violated the conjugal duties, prevented his adding anything further; he embraced his sweet child and, after saluting Matilda and me, hastily broke from us and, seating himself in his chaise, pursued the road to Aberdeen.

Never was there a better young man! Ah! how little did he deserve the misfortunes he has experienced in the marriage state. So good a husband to so bad a wife! For you know, my dear Charlotte, that the worthless Louisa left him, her child and reputation, a few weeks ago, in company with Danvers and dishonour. Never was there a sweeter face, a finer form, or a less amiable heart than Louisa owned! Her child already possesses the personal charms of her unhappy mother! May she inherit from her father all his mental ones!

Lesley is at present but five and twenty, and has already given himself up to melancholy and despair. What a difference between him and his father! Sir George is fifty-seven and still remains the beau, the flighty stripling, the gay lad, and sprightly youngster that his son was really about five years back, and that *he* has affected to appear ever since my remembrance.

While our father is fluttering about the streets of London gay, dissipated, and thoughtless at the age of fifty-seven, Matilda and I continue secluded from mankind in our old and mouldering castle which is situated two miles from Perth on a bold projecting rock, and commands an extensive view of the town and its delightful environs. But though retired from almost all the world – for we visit no one but the M'Leods, the M'Kenzies, the M'Phersons, the M'Cartneys, the M'Donalds, the M'kinnons, the M'lellans, the M'kays, the Macbeths and the Macduffs – we are neither dull nor unhappy; on the contrary there never were two more lively, more agreeable or more witty girls than we are; not an hour in the day hangs heavy on our hands.

We read, we work, we walk, and when fatigued with these employments, relieve our spirits either by a lively song, a graceful dance, or by some smart bon mot, and witty repartee. We are handsome, my dear Charlotte, very handsome and the greatest of our perfections is that we are entirely insensible of them ourselves.

But why do I thus dwell on myself! Let me rather repeat the praise of our dear little niece, the innocent Louisa, who is at present sweetly smiling in a gentle nap as she reposes on the sofa. The dear creature is just turned of two years old; as handsome as though two and twenty, as sensible as though two and thirty, and as prudent as though two and forty. To convince you of this, I must inform you that she has a very fine complexion and very pretty features, that she already knows the two first letters in the alphabet, and that she never tears her frocks. If I have not now convinced you of her beauty, sense and prudence, I have nothing more to urge in support of my assertion, and you will therefore have no way of deciding the affair but by coming to Lesley Castle, and by a personal acquaintance with Louisa, determine for yourself.

Ah! my dear friend, how happy should I be to see you within these venerable walls! It is now four years since my removal from school has separated me from you; that two such tender hearts, so closely linked together by the ties of sympathy and friendship, should be so widely removed from each other, is vastly moving. I live in Perthshire, you in Sussex. We might meet in London, were my father disposed to carry me there, and were your mother to be there at the same time. We might meet at Bath, at Tunbridge, or anywhere else indeed, could we but be at the same place together. We have only to hope that such a period may arrive. My father does not return to us till autumn; my brother will leave Scotland in a few days; he is impatient to travel. Mistaken youth! He vainly flatters himself that change of air will heal the wounds of a broken heart! You will join with me, I am certain, my dear Charlotte, in prayers for the recovery of the unhappy Lesley's peace of mind, which must ever be essential to that of your sincere friend

M. Lesley

Glenford
12th February

I have a thousand excuses to beg for having so long delayed thanking you, my dear Peggy, for your agreeable letter, which, believe me, I should not have deferred doing had not every moment of my time during the last five weeks been so fully employed in the necessary arrangements for my sister's wedding as to allow me no time to devote either to you or myself. And now what provokes me more than anything else is that the match is broke off, and all my labour thrown away.

Imagine how great the disappointment must be to me, when you consider that after having laboured both by night and by day in order to get the wedding dinner ready by the time appointed, after having roasted beef, broiled mutton, and stewed soup enough to last the new-married couple through the honeymoon, I had the mortification of finding that I had been roasting, broiling and stewing both the meat and myself to no purpose. Indeed, my dear friend, I never remember suffering any vexation equal to what I experienced on last Monday when my sister came running to me in the store room with her face as white as a whipped syllabub, and told me that Hervey had been thrown from his horse, had fractured his skull, and was pronounced by his surgeon to be in the most eminent danger.

'Good God!' said I, 'you don't say so? Why what in the name of heaven will become of all the victuals! We shall never be able to eat it while it is good. However, we'll call in the surgeon to help us. I shall be able to manage the sirloin myself, my mother will eat the soup, and you and the doctor must finish the rest.'

Here I was interrupted by seeing my poor sister fall down to appearance lifeless upon one of the chests where we keep our table linen. I immediately called my mother and the maids, and at last we brought her to herself again; as soon as ever she was sensible, she expressed a determination of going instantly to Henry, and was so wildly bent on this scheme that we had the greatest difficulty in the world to prevent her putting it in execution. At last, however, more by force than entreaty, we prevailed on her to go into her room; we laid her upon the bed, and she continued for some hours in the most dreadful convulsions.

My mother and I continued in the room with her, and when any intervals of tolerable composure in Eloisa would allow us, we joined in heartfelt lamentations on the dreadful waste in our provisions which this event must occasion, and in concerting some plan for getting rid of them. We agreed that the best thing we could do was to begin eating them immediately, and accordingly we ordered up the cold ham and fowls, and instantly began our devouring plan on them with great alacrity. We would have persuaded Eloisa to have taken a wing of a chicken, but she would not be persuaded.

She was, however, much quieter than she had been; the convulsions she had before suffered having given way to an almost perfect insensibility. We endeavoured to rouse her by every means in our power, but to no purpose. I talked to her of Henry. 'Dear Eloisa,' said I, 'there's no occasion for your crying so much about such a trifle' – for I was willing to make light of it in order to comfort her. 'I beg you would not mind it – you see it does not vex me in the least; though perhaps I may suffer most from it, after all; for I shall not only be obliged to eat up all the victuals I have dressed already, but must, if Henry should recover (which, however, is not very likely) dress as much for you again; or should he die (as I suppose he will) I shall still have to prepare a dinner for you whenever you marry anyone else. So you see that though perhaps for the present it may afflict you to think of Henry's sufferings, yet I dare say he'll die soon, and then his pain will be over and you will be easy, whereas my trouble will last much longer, for work as hard as I may, I am certain that the pantry cannot be cleared in less than a fortnight.'

Thus I did all in my power to console her, but without any effect, and at last, as I saw that she did not seem to listen to me, I said no more, but leaving her with my mother, I took down the remains of the ham and chicken, and sent William to ask how Henry did. He was not expected to live many hours; he died the same day.

We took all possible care to break the melancholy event to Eloisa in the tenderest manner; yet in spite of every precaution, her sufferings on hearing it were too violent for her reason, and she continued for many hours in a high delirium. She is still extremely ill, and her physicians are greatly afraid of her going into a decline. We are therefore preparing for Bristol, where we mean to be in the course of the next week.

And now, my dear Margaret, let me talk a little of your affairs; and in the first place I must inform you that it is confidently reported your father is going to be married. I am very unwilling to believe so unpleasing a report, and at the same time cannot wholly discredit it. I have written to my friend Susan Fitzgerald for information concerning it, which as she is at present in town, she will be very able to give me. I know not who is the lady.

I think your brother is extremely right in the resolution he has taken of travelling, as it will perhaps contribute to obliterate from his remembrance those disagreeable events which have lately so much afflicted him – I am happy to find that though secluded from all the world, neither you nor Matilda are dull or unhappy – that you may never know what it is to be either is the wish of your sincerely affectionate

C.L.

PS I have this instant received an answer from my friend Susan, which I enclose to you, and on which you will make your own reflections.

THE ENCLOSED LETTER

My dear Charlotte,
You could not have applied for information concerning the report of Sir George Lesley's marriage to anyone better able to give it you than I am. Sir George is certainly married; I was myself present at the ceremony, which you will not be surprised at when I subscribe myself your affectionate

Susan Lesley

LETTER THE THIRD
From Miss Margaret Lesley to Miss C. Lutterell

Lesley Castle
16th February

I *have* made my own reflections on the letter you enclosed to me, my dear Charlotte, and I will now tell you what those reflections were. I reflected that if by this second marriage Sir George should have a second family, our fortunes must be considerably diminished; that if his wife should be of an extravagant turn, she would encourage him to persevere in that gay and dissipated way of life to which little encouragement would be necessary, and which has, I fear, already proved but too detrimental to his health and fortune; that she would now become mistress of those jewels which once adorned our mother, and which Sir George had always promised us; that if they did not come into Perthshire I should not be able to gratify my curiosity of beholding my mother-in-law, and that if they did, Matilda would no longer sit at the head of her father's table.

These, my dear Charlotte, were the melancholy reflections which crowded into my imagination after perusing Susan's letter to you, and which instantly occurred to Matilda when she had perused it likewise. The same ideas, the same fears, immediately occupied her mind, and I know not which reflection distressed her most, whether the probable diminution of our fortunes, or her own consequence. We both wish very much to know whether Lady Lesley is handsome and what is your opinion of her; as you honour her with the appellation of your friend, we flatter ourselves that she must be amiable.

My brother is already in Paris. He intends to quit it in a few days, and to begin his route to Italy. He writes in a most cheerful manner, says that the air of France has greatly recovered both his health and spirits; that he has now entirely ceased to think of Louisa with any degree either of pity or affection; that he even feels himself obliged to her for her elopement, as he thinks it very good fun to be single again. By this, you may perceive that he has entirely regained that cheerful gaiety and sprightly wit for which he was once so remarkable.

When he first became acquainted with Louisa which was little more than three years ago, he was one of the most lively, the most agreeable young men of the age. I believe you never yet heard the particulars of his first acquaintance with her.

It commenced at our cousin Colonel Drummond's; at whose house in Cumberland he spent the Christmas in which he attained the age of two and twenty. Louisa Burton was the daughter of a distant relation of Mrs Drummond, who dying a few months before in extreme poverty, left his only child, then about eighteen, to the protection of any of his relations who would protect her. Mrs Drummond was the only one who found herself so disposed – Louisa was therefore removed from a miserable cottage in Yorkshire to an elegant mansion in Cumberland, and from every pecuniary distress that poverty could inflict, to every elegant enjoyment that money could purchase.

Louisa was naturally ill-tempered and cunning; but she had been taught to disguise her real disposition, under the appearance of insinuating sweetness, by a father who but too well knew that to be married would be the only chance she would have of not being starved, and who flattered himself that with such an extraordinary share of personal beauty,

11

joined to a gentleness of manners, and an engaging address, she might stand a good chance of pleasing some young man who might afford to marry a girl without a shilling. Louisa perfectly entered into her father's schemes and was determined to forward them with all her care and attention.

By dint of perseverance and application, she had at length so thoroughly disguised her natural disposition under the mask of innocence and softness as to impose upon everyone who had not by a long and constant intimacy with her discovered her real character. Such was Louisa when the hapless Lesley first beheld her at Drummond House.

His heart which – to use your favourite comparison – was as delicate, as sweet, and as tender as a whipped syllabub, could not resist her attractions. In a very few days, he was falling in love, shortly after actually fell, and before he had known her a month, he had married her. My father was at first highly displeased at so hasty and imprudent a connection; but when he found that they did not mind it, he soon became perfectly reconciled to the match.

The estate near Aberdeen which my brother possesses, by the bounty of his great uncle, independent of Sir George, was entirely sufficient to support him and my sister in elegance and ease. For the first twelvemonth, no one could be happier than Lesley, and no one more amiable to appearance than Louisa, and so plausibly did she act and so cautiously behave that though Matilda and I often spent several weeks together with them, yet we neither of us had any suspicion of her real disposition.

After the birth of Louisa, however – which one would have thought would have strengthened her regard for Lesley – the mask she had so long supported was by degrees thrown aside, and as probably she then thought herself secure in the affection of her husband (which did indeed appear if possible augmented by the birth of his child) she seemed to take no pains to prevent that affection from ever diminishing.

Our visits therefore to Dunbeath were now less frequent and by far less agreeable than they used to be. Our absence was, however, never either mentioned or lamented by Louisa who, in the society of young Danvers with whom she became acquainted at Aberdeen (he was at one of the universities there), felt infinitely happier than in that of Matilda and your friend, though there certainly never were pleasanter girls than we are.

You know the sad end of all Lesley's connubial happiness; I will not repeat it.

Adieu, my dear Charlotte; although I have not yet mentioned anything of the matter, I hope you will do me the justice to believe that I *think* and *feel* a great deal for your sister's affliction. I do not doubt but that the healthy air of the Bristol Downs will entirely remove it, by erasing from her mind the remembrance of Henry.

I am, my dear Charlotte, yours ever

M. L.

Bristol
27th February

My dear Peggy,

I have but just received your letter which, being directed to Sussex while I was at Bristol, was obliged to be forwarded to me here, and from some unaccountable delay, has but this instant reached me.

I return you many thanks for the account it contains of Lesley's acquaintance, love and marriage with Louisa, which has not the less entertained me for having often been repeated to me before.

I have the satisfaction of informing you that we have every reason to imagine our pantry is by this time nearly cleared, as we left particular orders with the servants to eat as hard as they possibly could, and to call in a couple of charwomen to assist them. We brought a cold pigeon pie, a cold turkey, a cold tongue, and half a dozen jellies with us, which we were lucky enough with the help of our landlady, her husband, and their three children, to get rid of in less than two days after our arrival.

Poor Eloisa is still so very indifferent both in health and spirits that I very much fear the air of the Bristol Downs, healthy as it is, has not been able to drive poor Henry from her remembrance.

You ask me whether your new mother-in-law is handsome and amiable – I will now give you an exact description of her bodily and mental charms. She is short, and extremely well made; is naturally pale, but rouges a good deal; has fine eyes, and fine teeth, as she will take care to let you know as soon as she sees you, and is altogether very pretty. She is remarkably good tempered when she has her own way, and very lively when she is not out of humour. She is naturally extravagant and not very affected; she never reads anything but the letters she receives from me, and never writes anything but her answers to them. She plays, sings and dances, but has no taste for either, and excels in none, though she says she is passionately fond of all.

Perhaps you may flatter me so far as to be surprised that one of whom I speak with so little affection should be my particular friend; but to tell you the truth, our friendship arose rather from caprice on her side than esteem on mine. We spent two or three days together with a lady in Berkshire with whom we both happened to be connected. During our visit – the weather being remarkably bad, and our party particularly stupid – she was so good as to conceive a violent partiality for me, which very soon settled in a downright friendship and ended in an established correspondence.

She is probably by this time as tired of me as I am of her; but as she is too polite and I am too civil to say so, our letters are still as frequent and affectionate as ever, and our attachment as firm and sincere as when it first commenced. As she had a great taste for the pleasures of London, and of Brighthelmstone[2], she will, I dare say, find some difficulty in prevailing on herself even to satisfy the curiosity I dare say she feels of beholding you, at the expense of quitting those favourite haunts of dissipation for the melancholy though venerable gloom of the castle you inhabit. Perhaps, however, if she finds her health impaired by too much amusement, she may acquire fortitude sufficient to undertake a journey to Scotland in the hope of its proving at least beneficial to her health, if not conducive to her happiness.

Your fears, I am sorry to say, concerning your father's extravagance, your own fortunes, your mother's jewels and your sister's consequence, I should suppose are but too well founded. My friend herself has four thousand pounds, and will probably spend nearly as much every year in dress and public places if she can get it – she will certainly not endeavour to reclaim Sir George from the manner of living to which he has been so long accustomed, and there is therefore some reason to fear that you will be very well off, if you get any fortune at all. The jewels, I should imagine, too, will undoubtedly be hers, and there is, too, much reason to think that she will preside at her husband's table in preference to his daughter. But as so melancholy a subject must necessarily extremely distress you, I will no longer dwell on it.

Eloisa's indisposition has brought us to Bristol at so unfashionable a season of the year that we have actually seen but one genteel family since we came. Mr and Mrs Marlowe are very agreeable people; the ill health of their little boy occasioned their arrival here; you may imagine that being the only family with whom we can converse, we are of course on a footing of intimacy with them; we see them indeed almost every day, and dined with them yesterday. We spent a very pleasant day, and had a very good dinner, though to be sure the veal was terribly underdone, and the curry had no seasoning. I could not help wishing all dinnertime that I had been at the dressing it.

A brother of Mrs Marlowe, Mr Cleveland, is with them at present; he is a good-looking young man, and seems to have a good deal to say for himself. I tell Eloisa that she should set her cap at him, but she does not at all seem to relish the proposal. I should like to see the girl married and Cleveland has a very good estate.

Perhaps you may wonder that I do not consider *myself* as well as my sister in my matrimonial projects; but to tell you the truth I never wish to act a more principal part at a wedding than the superintending and directing the dinner, and therefore while I can get any of my acquaintance to marry for me, I shall never think of doing it myself, as I very much suspect that I should not have so much time for dressing my own wedding dinner, as for dressing that of my friends.

Yours sincerely,

C.L.

Lesley Castle
18th March

On the same day that I received your last kind letter, Matilda received one from Sir George which was dated from Edinburgh, and informed us that he should do himself the pleasure of introducing Lady Lesley to us on the following evening. This, as you may suppose, considerably surprised us, particularly as your account of her ladyship had given us reason to imagine there was little chance of her visiting Scotland at a time that London must be so gay.

As it was our business, however, to be delighted at such a mark of condescension as a visit from Sir George and Lady Lesley, we prepared to return them an answer expressive of the happiness we enjoyed in expectation of such a blessing, when luckily recollecting that as they were to reach the castle the next evening, it would be impossible for my father to receive it before he left Edinburgh, we contented ourselves with leaving them to suppose that we were as happy as we ought to be.

At nine in the evening on the following day they came, accompanied by one of Lady Lesley's brothers. Her ladyship perfectly answers the description you sent me of her, except that I do not think her so pretty as you seem to consider her. She has not a bad face, but there is something so extremely unmajestic in her little diminutive figure as to render her, in comparison with the elegant height of Matilda and myself, an insignificant dwarf.

Her curiosity to see us (which must have been great to bring her more than four hundred miles) being now perfectly gratified, she already begins to mention their return to town, and has desired us to accompany her. We cannot refuse her request since it is seconded by the commands of our father, and thirded by the entreaties of Mr Fitzgerald who is certainly one of the most pleasing young men I ever beheld. It is not yet determined when we are to go, but whenever we do, we shall certainly take our little Louisa with us.

Adieu, my dear Charlotte; Matilda unites in best wishes to you, and Eloisa, with yours ever

M.L.

Lesley Castle
20th March

We arrived here, my sweet friend, about a fortnight ago, and I already heartily repent that I ever left our charming house in Portman Square for such a dismal old weather-beaten castle as this. You can form no idea sufficiently hideous of its dungeon-like form. It is actually perched upon a rock to appearance so totally inaccessible that I expected to have been pulled up by a rope; and sincerely repented having gratified my curiosity to behold my daughters at the expense of being obliged to enter their prison in so dangerous and ridiculous a manner.

But as soon as I once found myself safely arrived in the inside of this tremendous building, I comforted myself with the hope of having my spirits revived by the sight of two beautiful girls, such as the Miss Lesleys had been represented to me at Edinburgh. But here again, I met with nothing but disappointment and surprise. Matilda and Margaret Lesley are two great, tall, out-of-the-way, overgrown girls, just of a proper size to inhabit a castle almost as large in comparison as themselves.

I wish, my dear Charlotte, that you could but behold these Scotch giants; I am sure they would frighten you out of your wits. They will do very well as foils to myself, so I have invited them to accompany me to London where I hope to be in the course of a fortnight. Besides these two fair damsels, I found a little-humoured brat here who I believe is some relation to them; they told me who she was, and gave me a long rigmarole story of her father and a Miss *Somebody* which I have entirely forgot. I hate scandal and detest children. I have been plagued ever since I came here with tiresome visits from a parcel of Scotch wretches with terrible hard names; they were so civil, gave me so many invitations, and talked of coming again so soon that I could not help affronting them. I suppose I shall not see them any more, and yet as a family party we are so stupid, that I do not know what to do with myself. These girls have no music, but Scotch airs, no drawings but Scotch mountains, and no books but Scotch poems – and I hate everything Scotch. In general I can spend half the day at my toilet with a great deal of pleasure, but why should I dress here, since there is not a creature in the house whom I have any wish to please.

I have just had a conversation with my brother in which he has greatly offended me, and which as I have nothing more entertaining to send you I will gave you the particulars of.

You must know that I have for these four or five days past strongly suspected William of entertaining a partiality to my eldest daughter. I own, indeed, that had *I* been inclined to fall in love with any woman, I should not have made choice of Matilda Lesley for the object of my passion, for there is nothing I hate so much as a tall woman. But, however, there is no accounting for some men's taste, and as William is himself nearly six feet high, it is not wonderful that he should be partial to that height.

Now as I have a very great affection for my brother and should be extremely sorry to see him unhappy, which I suppose he means to be if he cannot marry Matilda, as moreover I know that his circumstances will not allow him to marry anyone without a fortune, and that Matilda's is entirely dependant on her father, who will neither have his own inclination nor my permission to give her anything at present,

I thought it would be doing a good-natured action by my brother to let him know as much, in order that he might choose for himself whether to conquer his passion, or love and despair.

Accordingly, finding myself this morning alone with him in one of the horrid old rooms of this castle, I opened the cause to him in the following manner:

'Well, my dear William, what do you think of these girls? For my part, I do not find them so plain as I expected: but perhaps you may think me partial to the daughters of my husband and perhaps you are right – they are indeed so very like Sir George that it is natural to think –'

'My dear Susan,' cried he, in a tone of the greatest amazement, 'you do not really think they bear the least resemblance to their father! He is so very plain! – but I beg your pardon – I had entirely forgotten to whom I was speaking –'

'Oh! pray don't mind me;' replied I, 'everyone knows Sir George is horribly ugly, and I assure you I always thought him a fright.'

'You surprise me extremely,' answered William, 'by what you say both with respect to Sir George and his daughters. You cannot think your husband so deficient in personal charms as you speak of, nor can you surely see any resemblance between him and the Miss Lesleys who are, in my opinion, perfectly unlike him and perfectly handsome.'

'If that is your opinion with regard to the girls, it certainly is no proof of their father's beauty, for if they are perfectly unlike him and very handsome at the same time, it is natural to suppose that he is very plain.'

'By no means,' said he, 'for what may be pretty in a woman, may be very unpleasing in a man.'

'But you yourself,' replied I, 'but a few minutes ago allowed him to be very plain.'

'Men are no judges of beauty in their own sex,' said he.

'Neither men nor women can think Sir George tolerable.'

'Well, well,' said he, 'we will not dispute about *his* beauty, but your opinion of his *daughters* is surely very singular, for if I understood you right, you said you did not find them so plain as you expected to do!'

'Why, do *you* find them plainer then?' said I.

'I can scarcely believe you to be serious,' returned he, 'when you speak of their persons in so extraordinary a manner. Do not you think the Miss Lesleys are two very handsome young women?'

'Lord! No!' cried I, 'I think them terribly plain!'

'Plain!' replied he. 'My dear Susan, you cannot really think so! Why, what single feature in the face of either of them can you possibly find fault with?'

'Oh! trust me for that,' replied I. 'Come, I will begin with the eldest – with Matilda. Shall I, William?' I looked as cunning as I could when I said it, in order to shame him.

'They are so much alike,' said he, 'that I should suppose the faults of one would be the faults of both.'

'Well, then, in the first place, they are both so horribly tall!'

'They are *taller* than you are indeed,' said he, with a saucy smile.

'Nay,' said I, 'I know nothing of that.'

'Well, but,' he continued, 'though they may be above the common size, their figures are perfectly elegant; and as to their faces, their eyes are beautiful.'

'I never can think such tremendous, knock-me-down figures in the least degree elegant; and as for their eyes, they are so tall that I never could strain my neck enough to look at them.'

'Nay,' replied he, 'I know not whether you may not be in the

23

right in not attempting it, for perhaps they might dazzle you with their lustre.'

'Oh! Certainly,' said I, with the greatest complacency, for I assure you, my dearest Charlotte, I was not in the least offended, though by what followed, one would suppose that William was conscious of having given me just cause to be so, for coming up to me and taking my hand, he said:

'You must not look so grave, Susan; you will make me fear I have offended you!'

'Offended me! Dear brother, how came such a thought in your head!' returned I. 'No, really! I assure you that I am not in the least surprised at your being so warm an advocate for the beauty of these girls –'

'Well, but,' interrupted William, 'remember that we have not yet concluded our dispute concerning them. What fault do you find with their complexion?'

'They are so horridly pale.'

'They have always a little colour, and after any exercise it is considerably heightened.'

'Yes, but if there should ever happen to be any rain in this part of the world, they will never be able raise more than their common stock – except, indeed, they amuse themselves with running up and down these horrid old galleries and antechambers.'

'Well,' replied my brother, in a tone of vexation and glancing an impertinent look at me, 'if they *have* but little colour, at least, it is all their own.'

This was too much, my dear Charlotte, for I am certain that he had the impudence by that look, of pretending to suspect the reality of mine. But you, I am sure, will vindicate my character whenever you may hear it so cruelly aspersed, for you can witness how often I have protested against wearing rouge, and how much I always told you I disliked it. And I assure you that my opinions are still the same.

Well, not bearing to be so suspected by my brother, I left the room immediately, and have been ever since in my own dressing room writing to you. What a long letter have I made of it! But you must not expect to receive such from me when I get to town, for it is only at Lesley Castle that one has time to write even to a Charlotte Lutterell.

I was so much vexed by William's glance that I could not summon patience enough to stay and give him that advice respecting his attachment to Matilda which had first induced me from pure love to him to begin the conversation; and I am now so thoroughly convinced by it, of his violent passion for her, that I am certain he would never hear reason on the subject, and I shall therefore give myself no more trouble either about him or his favourite.

Adieu, my dear girl –
Yours affectionately

Susan L.

LETTER THE SEVENTH
From Miss C. Lutterell to Miss M. Lesley

Bristol
27th March

I have received letters from you and your mother-in-law within this week which have greatly entertained me, as I find by them that you are both downright jealous of each other's beauty. It is very odd that two pretty women, though actually mother and daughter, cannot be in the same house without falling out about their faces. Do be convinced that you are both perfectly handsome and say no more of the matter.

I suppose this letter must be directed to Portman Square where probably – great as is your affection for Lesley Castle – you will not be sorry to find yourself. In spite of all that people may say about green fields and the country, I was always of the opinion that London and its amusements must be very agreeable for a while, and should be very happy could my mother's income allow her to jockey us into its public places during winter.

I always longed particularly to go to Vauxhall[3] to see whether the cold beef there is cut so thin as it is reported, for I have a sly suspicion that few people understand the art of cutting a slice of cold beef so well as I do: nay it would be hard if I did not know something of the matter, for it was a part of my education that I took by far the most pains with. Mama always found me *her* best scholar, though when Papa was alive Eloisa was *his*. Never, to be sure, were there two more different dispositions in the world. We both loved reading. *She* preferred histories, and *I* receipts. She loved drawing pictures, and I drawing pullets. No one could sing a better song than she, and no one make a better pie than I.

And so it has always continued since we have been no longer children. The only difference is that all disputes on the superior excellence of our employments *then* so frequent are now no more. We have for many years entered into an agreement always to admire each other's works; I never fail listening to *her* music, and she is as constant in eating *my* pies.

Such at least was the case till Henry Hervey made his appearance in Sussex. Before the arrival of his aunt in our neighbourhood where she established herself, you know, about a twelvemonth ago, his visits to her had been at stated times and of equal and settled duration; but on her removal to the Hall, which is within a walk from our house, they became both more frequent and longer.

This, as you may suppose, could not be pleasing to Mrs Diana who is a professed enemy to everything which is not directed by decorum and formality, or which bears the least resemblance to ease and good breeding. Nay, so great was her aversion to her nephew's behaviour that I have often heard her give such hints of it before his face that, had not Henry at such times been engaged in conversation with Eloisa, they must have caught his attention and have very much distressed him.

The alteration in my sister's behaviour which I have before hinted at, now took place. The agreement we had entered into of admiring each other's productions she no longer seemed to regard, and though I constantly applauded even every country dance she played, yet not even a pigeon pie of my making could obtain from her a single word of approbation. This was certainly enough to put anyone in a passion; however, I was as cool as a cream cheese and, having formed my plan and concerted a scheme of revenge, I was determined to let her have her own way and not even to make her a single reproach.

My scheme was to treat her as she treated me, and though she might even draw my own picture or play Malbrook[4] – which is the only tune I ever really liked – not to say so much as 'Thank you, Eloisa,' though I had for many years constantly hollowed whenever she played, '*bravo*', '*bravissimo*', '*encore*', '*da capo*', '*allegretto*', '*con expressione*', and '*poco presto*'[5] with many other such outlandish words, all of them as Eloisa told me expressive of my admiration. And so indeed I suppose they are, as I see some of them in every page of every music book, being the sentiments, I imagine, of the composer.

I executed my plan with great punctuality. I cannot say success, for alas! my silence while she played seemed not in the least to displease her; on the contrary she actually said to me one day, 'Well, Charlotte, I am very glad to find that you have at last left off that ridiculous custom of applauding my execution on the harpsichord till you made my head ache, and yourself hoarse. I feel very much obliged to you for keeping your admiration to yourself.'

I never shall forget the very witty answer I made to this speech.

'Eloisa,' said I, 'I beg you would be quite at your ease with respect to all such fears in future, for be assured that I shall always keep my admiration to myself and my own pursuits and never extend it to yours.'

This was the only very severe thing I ever said in my life; not but that I have often felt myself extremely satirical, but it was the only time I ever made my feelings public.

I suppose there never were two young people who had a greater affection for each other than Henry and Eloisa; no, the love of your brother for Miss Burton could not be so strong though it might be more violent. You may imagine, therefore, how provoked my sister must have been to have him play her such a trick. Poor girl! She still laments his death with un-diminished constancy, notwithstanding he has been dead more than six weeks; but some people mind such things more than others.

The ill state of health into which his loss has thrown her makes her so weak, and so unable to support the least exertion that she has been in tears all this morning merely from having taken leave of Mrs Marlowe who with her husband, brother and child are to leave Bristol this morning. I am sorry to have them go because they are the only family with whom we have here any acquaintance, but I never thought of crying; to be sure Eloisa and Mrs Marlowe have always been more together than with me, and have therefore contracted a kind of affection for each other which does not make tears so inexcusable in them as they would be in me.

The Marlowes are going to town; Cleveland accompanies them; as neither Eloisa nor I could catch him I hope you or Matilda may have better luck.

I know not when we shall leave Bristol. Eloisa's spirits are so low that she is very averse to moving, and yet is certainly by no means mended by her residence here. A week or two will, I hope, determine our measures.

In the meantime, believe me and etc., etc.

Charlotte Lutterell

LETTER THE EIGHTH
Miss Lutterell to Mrs Marlowe

Bristol
4th April

I feel myself greatly obliged to you, my dear Emma, for such a mark of your affection as I flatter myself was conveyed in the proposal you made me of our corresponding; I assure you that it will be a great relief to me to write to you, and as long as my health and spirits will allow me, you will find me a very *constant* correspondent; I will not say an entertaining one, for you know my situation sufficiently not to be ignorant that in me mirth would be improper, and I know my own heart too well not to be sensible that it would be unnatural. You must not expect news, for we see no one with whom we are in the least acquainted, or in whose proceedings we have any interest. You must not expect scandal, for by the same rule we are equally debarred either from hearing or inventing it. – You must expect from me nothing but the melancholy effusions of a broken heart which is ever reverting to the happiness it once enjoyed and which ill supports its present wretchedness.

The possibility of being able to write, to speak, to you of my lost Henry will be a luxury to me, and your goodness will not, I know, refuse to read what it will so much relieve my heart to write. I once thought that to have what is in general called a friend – I mean one of my own sex to whom I might speak with less reserve than to any other person – independent of my sister, would never be an object of my wishes, but how much was I mistaken! Charlotte is too much engrossed by two confidential correspondents of that sort to supply the place of one to me, and I hope you will not think me girlishly romantic when I say that to have some kind and compassionate friend who might listen to my sorrows without endeavouring to console me was what I had for some time wished for, when our acquaintance with you, the intimacy which followed it and the particular affectionate attention you paid me almost from the first, caused me to entertain the flattering idea of those attentions being improved on a closer acquaintance into a friendship which, if you were what my wishes formed you, would be the greatest happiness I could be capable of enjoying.

To find that such hopes are realised is a satisfaction indeed; a satisfaction which is now almost the only one I can ever experience. I feel myself so languid that I am sure, were you with me, you would oblige me to leave off writing, and I cannot give you a greater proof of my affection for you than by acting, as I know you would wish me to do, whether absent or present.

I am, my dear, Emma's sincere friend

E.L.

LETTER THE NINTH
Mrs Marlowe to Miss Lutterell

Grosvenor Street
10th April

Need I say, my dear Eloisa, how welcome your letter was to me. I cannot give a greater proof of the pleasure I received from it, or of the desire I feel that our correspondence may be regular and frequent than by setting you so good an example as I now do in answering it before the end of the week.

But do not imagine that I claim any merit in being so punctual; on the contrary I assure you that it is a far greater gratification to me to write to you than to spend the evening either at a concert or a ball. Mr Marlowe is so desirous of my appearing at some of the public places every evening that I do not like to refuse him, but at the same time so much wish to remain at home that, independent of the pleasure I experience in devoting any portion of my time to my dear Eloisa, yet the liberty I claim from having a letter to write of spending an evening at home with my little boy, you know me well enough to be sensible, will of itself be a sufficient inducement (if one is necessary) to my maintaining with pleasure a correspondence with you.

As to the subject of your letters to me, whether grave or merry, if they concern you they must be equally interesting to me; not but that I think the melancholy indulgence of your own sorrows by repeating them and dwelling on them to me will only encourage and increase them, and that it will be more prudent in you to avoid so sad a subject; but yet, knowing as I do what a soothing and melancholy pleasure it must afford you, I cannot prevail on myself to deny you so great an indulgence, and will only insist on your not expecting me to encourage you in it by my own letters. On the contrary, I intend to fill them with such lively wit and enlivening humour as shall even provoke a smile in the sweet but sorrowful countenance of my Eloisa.

In the first place, you are to learn that I have met your sister's three friends, Lady Lesley and her daughters, twice in public since I have been here. I know you will be impatient to hear my opinion of the beauty of three ladies of whom you have heard so much. Now, as you are too ill and too unhappy to be vain, I think I may venture to inform you that I like none of their faces so well as I do your own. Yet they are all handsome – Lady Lesley, indeed, I have seen before; her daughters I believe would, in general, be said to have a finer face than her ladyship, and yet what with the charms of a blooming complexion, a little affectation and a great deal of small talk (in each of which she is superior to the young ladies), she will, I dare say, gain herself as many admirers as the more regular features of Matilda and Margaret.

I am sure you will agree with me in saying that they can none of them be of a proper size for real beauty, when you know that two of them are taller and the other shorter than ourselves. In spite of this defect – or rather by reason of it – there is something very noble and majestic in the figures of the Miss Lesleys, and something agreeably lively in the appearance of their pretty little mother-in-law.

But though one may be majestic and the other lively, yet the faces of neither possess that bewitching sweetness of my Eloisa's, which her present languor is so far from diminishing.

What would my husband and brother say of us if they knew all the fine things I have been saying to you in this letter! It is very hard that a pretty woman is never to be told she is so by anyone of her own sex without that person's being suspected to be either her determined enemy, or her professed toad eater. How much more amiable are women in that particular! One man may say forty civil things to another without our supposing that he is ever paid for it, and provided he does his duty by our sex, we care not how polite he is to his own.

Mrs Lutterell will be so good as to accept my compliments; Charlotte, my love; and Eloisa, the best wishes for the recovery of her health and spirits that can be offered by her affectionate friend

E. Marlowe.

I am afraid this letter will be but a poor specimen of my powers in the witty way; and your opinion of them will not be greatly increased when I assure you that I have been as entertaining as I possibly could.

LETTER THE TENTH
From Miss Margaret Lesley to Miss Charlotte Lutterell

Portman Square
13th April

My dear Charlotte,

We left Lesley Castle on the twenty-eighth of last month, and arrived safely in London after a journey of seven days. I had the pleasure of finding your letter here waiting my arrival, for which you have my grateful thanks.

Ah! my dear friend, I every day more regret the serene and tranquil pleasures of the castle we have left in exchange for the uncertain and unequal amusements of this vaunted city. Not that I will pretend to assert that these uncertain and unequal amusements are in the least degree unpleasing to me; on the contrary I enjoy them extremely and should enjoy them even more, were I not certain that every appearance I make in public but rivets the chains of those unhappy beings whose passion it is impossible not to pity, though it is out of my power to return.

In short, my dear Charlotte, it is my sensibility for the sufferings of so many amiable young men, my dislike of the extreme admiration I meet with, and my aversion to being so celebrated both in public, in private, in papers, and in print shops, that are the reasons why I cannot more fully enjoy the amusements so various and pleasing of London.

How often have I wished that I possessed as little personal beauty as you do; that my figure were as inelegant; my face as unlovely; and my appearance as unpleasing as yours! But ah! what little chance is there of so desirable an event. I have had the smallpox, and must therefore submit to my unhappy fate.

I am now going to entrust you, my dear Charlotte, with a secret which has long disturbed the tranquillity of my days, and which is of a kind to require the most inviolable secrecy from you.

Last Monday se'night Matilda and I accompanied Lady Lesley to a rout at the Honourable Mrs Kickabout's. We were escorted by Mr Fitzgerald who is a very amiable young man in the main, though perhaps a little singular in his taste – he is in love with Matilda. We had scarcely paid our compliments to the lady of the house and curtsied to half a score different people when my attention was attracted by the appearance of a young man the most lovely of his sex, who at that moment entered the room with another gentleman and lady. From the first moment I beheld him, I was certain that on him depended the future happiness of my life.

Imagine my surprise when he was introduced to me by the name of Cleveland! I instantly recognised him as the brother of Mrs Marlowe, and the acquaintance of my Charlotte at Bristol. Mr and Mrs M. were the gentleman and lady who accompanied him. (You do not think Mrs Marlowe handsome?) The elegant address of Mr Cleveland, his polished manners and delightful bow at once confirmed my attachment. He did not speak; but I can imagine everything he would have said had he opened his mouth. I can picture to myself the cultivated understanding, the noble sentiments, and elegant language which would have shone so conspicuous in the conversation of Mr Cleveland.

The approach of Sir James Gower – one of my too numerous admirers – prevented the discovery of any such powers by putting an end to a conversation we had never commenced, and by attracting my attention to himself. But oh! how inferior are the accomplishments of Sir James to those of his so greatly envied rival!

Sir James is one of the most frequent of our visitors, and is almost always of our parties. We have since often met Mr and Mrs Marlowe, but no Cleveland – he is always engaged somewhere else. Mrs Marlowe fatigues me to death every time I see her by her tiresome conversations about you and Eloisa. She is so stupid! I live in the hope of seeing her irresistible brother tonight as we are going to Lady Flambeau's who is, I know, intimate with the Marlowes.

Our party will be Lady Lesley, Matilda, Fitzgerald, Sir James Gower, and myself. We see little of Sir George, who is almost always at the gaming table. Ah! my poor Fortune, where art thou by this time? We see more of Lady L. who always makes her appearance (highly rouged) at dinner time. Alas! what delightful jewels will she be decked in this evening at Lady Flambeau's! Yet I wonder how she can herself delight in wearing them; surely she must be sensible of the ridiculous impropriety of loading her little diminutive figure with such superfluous ornaments. Is it possible that she cannot know how greatly superior an elegant simplicity is to the most studied apparel? Would she but present them to Matilda and me, how greatly should we be obliged to her, how becoming would diamonds be on our fine majestic figures! And how surprising it is that such an idea should never have occurred to *her*. I am sure if I have reflected in this manner once, I have fifty times. Whenever I see Lady Lesley dressed in them such reflections immediately come across me. My own mother's jewels too!

But I will say no more on so melancholy a subject – let me entertain you with something more pleasing. Matilda had a letter this morning from Lesley, by which we have the pleasure of finding that he is at Naples, has turned Roman Catholic, obtained one of the Pope's bulls for annulling his first marriage,[6] and has since actually married a Neapolitan lady of great rank and fortune. He tells us, moreover, that much the same sort of affair has befallen his first wife, the worthless Louisa, who is likewise at Naples, had turned Roman Catholic, and is soon to be married to a Neapolitan nobleman of great and distinguished merit. He says that they are at present very good friends, have quite forgiven all past errors, and intend in future to be very good neighbours. He invites Matilda and me to pay him a visit to Italy and to bring him his little Louisa, whom both her mother, step-mother, and himself are equally desirous of beholding.

As to our accepting his invitation, it is at present very uncertain: Lady Lesley advises us to go without loss of time; Fitzgerald offers to escort us there; but Matilda has some doubts of the propriety of such a scheme – she owns it would be very agreeable. I am certain she likes the fellow. My father desires us not to be in a hurry, as perhaps if we wait a few months both he and Lady Lesley will do themselves the pleasure of attending us. Lady Lesley says no, that nothing will ever tempt her to forego the amusements of Brighthelmstone for a journey to Italy merely to see our brother. 'No,' says the disagreeable woman, 'I have once in my life been fool enough to travel I don't know how many hundred miles to see two of the family, and I found it did not answer, so deuce take me if ever I am so foolish again.' So says her ladyship, but Sir George still perseveres in saying that perhaps, in a month or two, they may accompany us.

Adieu, my dear Charlotte.

Your faithful,

Margaret Lesley

The History of England

FROM THE REIGN OF HENRY IV
TO THE DEATH OF CHARLES I[1]

BY A PARTIAL, PREJUDICED, AND
IGNORANT HISTORIAN[2]

To Miss Austen[3], eldest daughter of the Revd George Austen[4], this work is inscribed with all due respect by the Author.

NB There will be very few dates in this History.[5]

HENRY IV

Henry IV ascended the throne of England much to his own satisfaction in the year 1399, after having prevailed on his cousin and predecessor, Richard II, to resign it to him, and to retire for the rest of his life to Pomfret Castle, where he happened to be murdered. It is to be supposed that Henry was married, since he had certainly four sons, but it is not in my power to inform the reader who was his wife. Be this as it may, he did not live for ever, but falling ill, his son, the Prince of Wales, came and took away the Crown; whereupon the King made a long speech, for which I must refer the reader to Shakespeare's plays, and the Prince made a still longer. Things being thus settled between them, the King died, and was succeeded by his son Henry who had previously beaten Sir William Gascoigne[6].

HENRY V

This Prince, after he succeeded to the throne, grew quite reformed and amiable, forsaking all his dissipated companions, and never thrashing Sir William again. During his reign, Lord Cobham[7] was burnt alive, but I forget what for. His Majesty then turned his thoughts to France, where he went and fought the famous Battle of Agincourt. He afterwards married the King's daughter Catherine, a very agreeable woman by Shakespeare's account. In spite of all this, however, he died, and was succeeded by his son Henry.

HENRY VI

I cannot say much for this monarch's sense. Nor would I if I could, for he was a Lancastrian. I suppose you know all about the wars between him and the Duke of York who was of the right side; if you do not, you had better read some other history, for I shall not be very diffuse in this, meaning by it only to vent my spleen *against*, and show my hatred *to* all those people whose parties or principles do not suit with mine, and not to give information. This King married Margaret of Anjou, a woman whose distresses and misfortunes were so great as almost to make me, who hates her, pity her. It was in this reign that Joan of Arc lived and made such a *row* among the English. They should not have burnt her – but they did. There were several battles between the Yorkists and Lancastrians, in which the former (as they ought) usually conquered. At length they were entirely overcome; the King was murdered; the Queen was sent home – and Edward IV ascended the throne.

EDWARD IV

This monarch was famous only for his beauty and his courage, of which the picture we have here given of him, and his undaunted behaviour in marrying one woman while he was engaged to another, are sufficient proofs. His wife was Elizabeth Woodville, a widow who – poor woman! – was afterwards confined in a convent by that monster of iniquity and avarice, Henry VII. One of Edward's mistresses was Jane Shore, who has had a play written about her, but it is a tragedy and therefore not worth reading.[8] Having performed all these noble actions, His Majesty died, and was succeeded by his son.

EDWARD V

This unfortunate Prince lived so little a while that nobody had time to draw his picture. He was murdered by his uncle's contrivance, whose name was Richard III.

RICHARD III

The character of this Prince has been in general very severely treated by historians,[9] but as he was a *York*, I am rather inclined to suppose him a very respectable man. It has indeed been confidently asserted that he killed his two nephews and his wife, but it has also been declared that he did not kill his two nephews, which I am inclined to believe true; and if this is the case, it may also be affirmed that he did not kill his wife, for if Perkin Warbeck was really the Duke of York, why might not Lambert Simnel be the widow of Richard.[10] Whether innocent or guilty, he did not reign long in peace, for Henry Tudor, Earl of Richmond, as great a villain as ever lived, made a great fuss about getting the Crown and, having killed the King at the Battle of Bosworth, he succeeded to it.

HENRY VII

This monarch, soon after his accession, married the Princess Elizabeth of York, by which alliance he plainly proved that he thought his own right inferior to hers, though he pretended to the contrary. By this marriage he had two sons and two daughters, the elder of which daughters was married to the King of Scotland and had the happiness of being grandmother to one of the first characters in the world.[11] But of *her*, I shall have occasion to speak more at large in future. The youngest, Mary, married first the King of France, and secondly the Duke of Suffolk, by whom she had one daughter, afterwards the mother of Lady Jane Grey, who, though inferior to her lovely cousin the Queen of Scots, was yet an amiable young woman and famous for reading Greek while other people were hunting. It was in the reign of Henry VII that Perkin Warbeck and Lambert Simnel before mentioned made their appearance: the former of whom was set in the stocks, took shelter in Beaulieu Abbey, and was beheaded with the Earl of Warwick; and the latter was taken into the King's kitchen. His Majesty died and was succeeded by his son Henry, whose only merit was his not being *quite* so bad as his daughter Elizabeth.

HENRY VIII

It would be an affront to my readers were I to suppose that they were not as well acquainted with the particulars of this King's reign as I am myself. It will therefore be saving *them* the task of reading again what they have read before, and *myself* the trouble of writing what I do not perfectly recollect, by giving only a slight sketch of the principal events which marked his reign. Among these may be ranked Cardinal Wolsey's telling the Father Abbott of Leicester Abbey that 'he was come to lay his bones among them',[12] the Reformation in religion, and the King's riding through the streets of London with Anne Boleyn. It is, however, but justice and my duty to declare that this amiable woman was entirely innocent of the crimes with which she was accused, and of which her beauty, her elegance, and her sprightliness were sufficient proofs, not to mention her solemn protestations of innocence, the weakness of the charges against her, and the King's character; all of which add some confirmation, though perhaps but slight ones when in comparison with those before alleged in her favour. Though I do not profess giving many dates, yet as I think it proper to give some, and shall of course make choice of those which it is most necessary for the reader to know, I think it right to inform him that her letter to the King was dated on the 6th of May.[13] The crimes and cruelties of this Prince were too numerous to be mentioned – as this history, I trust, has fully shown – and nothing can be said in his vindication, but that his abolishing religious houses and leaving them to the ruinous depredations of time has been of infinite use to the landscape of England in general, which probably was a principal motive for his doing it, since otherwise why should a man who was of no religion himself be at so much trouble to abolish one which had for ages been established in the kingdom.

His Majesty's fifth wife was the Duke of Norfolk's niece who, though universally acquitted of the crimes for which she was beheaded, has been by many people supposed to have led an abandoned life before her marriage – of this, however, I have many doubts, since she was a relation of that noble Duke of Norfolk who was so warm in the Queen of Scotland's cause, and who at last fell a victim to it.

The King's last wife contrived to survive him, but with difficulty effected it. He was succeeded by his only son Edward.

EDWARD VI

As this Prince was only nine years old at the time of his father's death, he was considered by many people as too young to govern, and the late King, happening to be of the same opinion, his mother's brother, the Duke of Somerset, was chosen Protector of the Realm during his minority. This man was, on the whole, of a very amiable character, and is somewhat of a favourite with me, though I would by no means pretend to affirm that he was equal to those first of men, Robert Earl of Essex, Delamere, or Gilpin.[14] He was beheaded, of which he might with reason have been proud, had he known that such was the death of Mary Queen of Scotland; but as it was impossible that he should be conscious of what had never happened, it does not appear that he felt particularly delighted with the manner of it. After his decease the Duke of Northumberland had the care of the King and the kingdom, and performed his trust of both so well that the King died and the kingdom was left to his daughter-in-law, the Lady Jane Grey, who has been already mentioned as reading Greek. Whether she really understood that language or whether such a study proceeded only from an excess of vanity for which I believe she was always rather remarkable, is uncertain. Whatever might be the cause, she preserved the same appearance of knowledge – and contempt of what was generally esteemed pleasure – during the whole of her life, for she declared herself displeased with being appointed queen, and while conducting to the scaffold, she wrote a sentence in Latin and another in Greek on seeing the dead body of her husband accidentally passing that way.

MARY

This woman had the good luck of being advanced to the throne of England in spite of the superior pretensions, merit and *beauty* of her cousins Mary Queen of Scotland and Jane Grey. Nor can I pity the kingdom for the misfortunes they experienced during her reign, since they fully deserved them for having allowed her to succeed her brother – which was a double piece of folly since they might have foreseen that, as she died without children, she would be succeeded by that disgrace to humanity, that pest of society, Elizabeth. Many were the people who fell martyrs to the Protestant religion during her reign; I suppose not fewer than a dozen. She married Philip King of Spain who, in her sister's reign, was famous for building Armadas. She died without issue, and then the dreadful moment came in which the destroyer of all comfort, the deceitful betrayer of trust reposed in her, and the murderess of her cousin succeeded to the throne.

It was the peculiar misfortune of this woman to have bad ministers – since wicked as she herself was, she could not have committed such extensive mischief had not these vile and abandoned men connived at and encouraged her in her crimes. I know that it has by many people been asserted and believed that Lord Burleigh, Sir Francis Walsingham, and the rest of those who filled the chief offices of State were deserving, experienced and able ministers. But oh! how blinded such writers and such readers must be to true merit, to merit despised, neglected and defamed, if they can persist in such opinions when they reflect that these men – these boasted men – were such scandals to their country and their sex as to allow and assist their Queen in confining for the space of nineteen years, a *woman* who, if the claims of relationship and merit were of no avail, yet as a Queen and as one who condescended to place confidence in her, had every reason to expect assistance and protection; and at length in allowing Elizabeth to bring this amiable woman to an untimely, unmerited, and scandalous death. Can anyone, if he reflects but for a moment on this blot, this everlasting blot upon their understanding and their character, allow any praise to Lord Burleigh or Sir Francis Walsingham? Oh! what must this bewitching Princess, whose only friend was then the Duke of Norfolk – and whose only ones now Mr Whitaker, Mrs Lefroy, Mrs Knight and myself[15] – who was abandoned by her son, confined by her cousin, abused, reproached and vilified by all, what must not her most noble mind have suffered when informed that Elizabeth had given orders for her death! Yet she bore it with a most unshaken fortitude, firm in her mind; constant in her religion; and prepared herself to meet the cruel fate to which she was doomed, with a magnanimity that could alone proceed from conscious innocence. And yet could you, Reader, have believed it possible that some hardened and zealous Protestants have even abused her for that steadfastness in the Catholic religion which reflected on her so much credit? But this is a striking proof of *their* narrow souls and prejudiced judgements who accuse her. She was executed in the Great Hall at Fotheringay Castle (sacred place!) on Wednesday 8th February 1587 – to the everlasting reproach of Elizabeth, her ministers, and of England in general. It may not be unnecessary before I entirely conclude my account of this ill-fated Queen, to observe that she had been accused of several crimes during the time of her reigning in Scotland, of which I now most seriously do assure my reader that she was entirely innocent; having never been guilty of anything more than imprudencies into which she was betrayed by the openness of her heart, her youth, and her education. Having I trust, by this assurance, entirely done away every suspicion and every doubt which might have arisen in the reader's mind from what other historians have written of her, I shall proceed to mention the remaining events that marked Elizabeth's reign. It was about this time that Sir Francis Drake, the first English navigator who sailed round the world, lived, to be the ornament of his country and his profession. Yet great as he was, and justly celebrated as a sailor, I cannot help foreseeing that he will be equalled, in this or the next century, by one who, though now but young, already promises to answer all the ardent and sanguine expectations of his relations and friends, amongst whom I may class the amiable lady to whom this work is dedicated, and my no less amiable self.[16]

Though of a different profession, and shining in a different sphere of life, yet equally conspicuous in the character of an *earl* as Drake was in that of a *sailor*, was Robert Devereux, Lord Essex. This unfortunate young man was not unlike in character to that equally unfortunate one *Frederic Delamere*. The simile may be carried still further, and Elizabeth – the torment of Essex – may be compared to the Emmeline of Delamere. It would be endless to recount the misfortunes of this noble and gallant earl. It is sufficient to say that he was beheaded on 25th February, after having been Lord Lieutenant of Ireland, after having clapped his hand on his sword, and after performing many other services to his country. Elizabeth did not long survive his loss, and died so miserable that, were it not an injury to the memory of Mary, I should pity her.

JAMES I

Though this King had some faults, among which and as the most principal, was his allowing his mother's death, yet considered on the whole I cannot help liking him. He married Anne of Denmark, and had several children; fortunately for him his eldest son, Prince Henry, died before his father or he might have experienced the evils which befell his unfortunate brother.

As I am myself partial to the Roman Catholic religion, it is with infinite regret that I am obliged to blame the behaviour of any member of it: yet truth being, I think, very excusable in a historian, I am necessitated to say that in this reign the Roman Catholics of England did not behave like gentlemen to the Protestants. Their behaviour, indeed, to the Royal family and both Houses of Parliament might justly be considered by them as very uncivil, and even Sir Henry Percy, though certainly the best bred man of the party, had none of that general politeness which is so universally pleasing, as his attentions were entirely confined to Lord Mounteagle.[17]

Sir Walter Raleigh flourished in this and the preceding reign, and is by many people held in great veneration and respect – but as he was an enemy of the noble Essex, I have nothing to say in praise of him, and must refer all those who may wish to be acquainted with the particulars of his life, to Mr Sheridan's play of the *Critic*[18] where they will find many interesting anecdotes, as well of him as of his friend Sir Christopher Hatton.

His Majesty was of that amiable disposition which inclines to friendship, and in such points was possessed of a keener penetration in discovering merit than many other people. I once heard an excellent charade on a carpet, of which the subject I am now on reminds me, and as I think it may afford my readers some amusement to *find it out*, I shall here take the liberty of presenting it to them.

CHARADE

My first is what my second was to King James I,
and you tread on my whole.

The principal favourites of His Majesty were Car, who was afterwards created Earl of Somerset, and whose name, perhaps, may have some share in the above-mentioned charade, and George Villiers, afterwards Duke of Buckingham.

On His Majesty's death he was succeeded by his son Charles.

CHARLES I

This amiable monarch seems born to have suffered misfortunes equal to those of his lovely grandmother; misfortunes which he could not deserve since he was her descendant. Never certainly were there before so many detestable characters at one time in England as in this period of its history; never were amiable men so scarce. The number of them throughout the whole kingdom amounting only to *five*, besides the inhabitants of Oxford, who were always loyal to their king and faithful to his interests. The names of this noble five who never forgot the duty of the subject, or swerved from their attachment to His Majesty, were as follows: the King himself, ever steadfast in his own support,

Archbishop Laud, Earl of Strafford, Viscount Faulkland and Duke of Ormond, who were scarcely less strenuous or zealous in the cause. While the *villains* of the time would make too long a list to be written or read, I shall therefore content myself with mentioning the leaders of the gang: Cromwell, Fairfax, Hampden and Pym may be considered as the original causers of all the disturbances, distresses, and civil wars in which England for many years was embroiled. In this reign, as well as in that of Elizabeth, I am obliged, in spite of my attachment to the Scotch, to consider them as equally guilty with the generality of the English, since they dared to think differently from their sovereign, to forget the adoration which, as *Stuarts*, it was their duty to pay them, to rebel against, dethrone and imprison the unfortunate Mary; to oppose, to deceive, and to sell the no less unfortunate Charles. The events of this monarch's reign are too numerous for my pen, and indeed the recital of any events (except what I make myself) is uninteresting to me; my principal reason for undertaking the history of England being to prove the innocence of the Queen of Scotland, which I flatter myself with having effectually done, and to abuse Elizabeth, though I am rather fearful of having fallen short in the latter part of my scheme. As therefore it is not my intention to give any particular account of the distresses into which this King was involved through the misconduct and cruelty of his Parliament, I shall satisfy myself with vindicating him from the reproach of arbitrary and tyrannical government with which he has often been charged. This, I feel, is not difficult to be done, for with one argument I am certain of satisfying every sensible and well-disposed person whose opinions have been properly guided by a good education – and this argument is that he was a *Stuart*.

Catharine,
or The Bower

To Miss Austen[1]

Madam, encouraged by your warm patronage of 'The Beautiful Cassandra'[2]*, and 'The History of England', which through your generous support, have obtained a place in every library in the kingdom, and run through threescore editions, I take the liberty of begging the same exertions in favour of the following novel, which I humbly flatter myself, possesses merit beyond any already published, or any that will ever in future appear, except such as may proceed from the pen of your most grateful humble servant,*
the author

Steventon,
August 1792

Catharine had the misfortune, as many heroines have had before her, of losing her parents when she was very young, and of being brought up under the care of a maiden aunt who, while she tenderly loved her, watched over her conduct with so scrutinising a severity as to make it very doubtful to many people, and to Catharine amongst the rest, whether she loved her or not. She had frequently been deprived of a real pleasure through this jealous caution, had been sometimes obliged to relinquish a ball because an officer was to be there, or to dance with a partner of her aunt's introduction in preference to one of her own choice. But her spirits were naturally good and not easily depressed, and she possessed such a fund of vivacity and good humour as could only be damped by some very serious vexation.

Besides these antidotes against every disappointment, and consolations under them, she had another, which afforded her constant relief in all her misfortunes, and that was a fine shady bower, the work of her own infantine labours, assisted by those of two young companions who had resided in the same village. To this bower, which terminated a very pleasant and retired walk in her aunt's garden, she always wandered whenever anything disturbed her, and it possessed such a charm over her senses as constantly to tranquillise her mind and quiet her spirits. Solitude and reflection might perhaps have had the same effect in her bedchamber, yet habit had so strengthened the idea which fancy had first suggested, that such a thought never occurred to Kitty who was firmly persuaded that her bower alone could restore her to herself.

Her imagination was warm, and in her friendships, as well as in the whole tenure of her mind, she was enthusiastic. This beloved bower had been the united work of herself and two amiable girls, for whom, since her earliest years, she had felt the tenderest regard. They were the daughters of the clergyman of the parish with whose family, while it had continued there, her aunt had been on the most intimate terms, and the little girls, though separated for the greatest part of the year by the different modes of their education, were constantly together during the holidays of the Miss Wynnes. In those days of happy childhood, now so often regretted by Kitty, this arbour had been formed, and, separated perhaps for ever from these dear friends, it encouraged more than any other place the tender and melancholy recollections of hours rendered pleasant by them, at once so sorrowful, yet so soothing!

It was now two years since the death of Mr Wynne and the consequent dispersion of his family who had been left by it in great distress. They had been reduced to a state of absolute dependence on some relations, who though very opulent and very nearly connected with them, had with difficulty been prevailed on to contribute anything towards their support. Mrs Wynne was fortunately spared the knowledge and participation of their distress, by her release from a painful illness a few months before the death of her husband. The eldest daughter had been obliged to accept the offer of one of her cousins to equip her for the East Indies, and though infinitely against her inclinations, had been necessitated to embrace the only possibility that was offered to her of a maintenance. Yet it was one so opposite to all her ideas of propriety, so contrary to her wishes, so repugnant to her feelings, that she would almost have preferred servitude to it, had choice been allowed her. Her personal attractions had gained her a husband as soon as she had arrived at Bengal, and she had now been married nearly a twelvemonth. Splendidly, yet unhappily married; united to a man of double her own age, whose disposition was not amiable, and whose manners were unpleasing, though his character was respectable. Kitty had heard twice from her friend since her marriage, but her letters were always unsatisfactory, and though she did not openly avow her feelings, yet every line proved her to be unhappy. She spoke with pleasure of nothing, but of those amusements which they had shared together and which could return no more, and seemed to have no happiness in view but that of returning to England again.

Her sister had been taken by another relation, the dowager Lady Halifax, as a companion to her daughters, and had accompanied her family into Scotland about the same time of Cecilia's leaving England. From Mary therefore Kitty had the power of hearing more frequently, but her letters were scarcely more comfortable. There was not indeed that hopelessness of sorrow in her situation as in her sister's – she was not married, and could yet look forward to a change in her circumstances. But situated for the present without any immediate hope of it, in a family where, though all were her relations, she had no friend, she wrote usually in depressed spirits, which her separation from her sister and her sister's marriage had greatly contributed to make so.

Divided thus from the two she loved best on earth, while Cecilia and Mary were still more endeared to her by their loss, everything that brought a remembrance of them was doubly cherished, and the shrubs they had planted, and the keep-sakes they had given were rendered sacred. The living of Chetwynde was now in the possession of a Mr Dudley whose family, unlike the Wynnes, were productive only of vexation and trouble to Mrs Percival and her niece. Mr Dudley, who was the younger son of a very noble family – of a family more famed for their pride than their opulence – tenacious of his dignity, and jealous of his rights, was forever quarrelling, if not with Mrs Percival herself, with her steward and tenants concerning tithes, and with the principal neighbours themselves concerning the respect and parade he exacted. His wife, an ill-educated, untaught woman of ancient family, was proud of that family almost without knowing why, and like him too was haughty and quarrelsome, without considering for what. Their only daughter, who inherited the ignorance, the insolence, and pride of her parents, was, from that beauty of which she was unreasonably vain, considered by them as an irresistible creature, and looked up to as the future restorer, by a splendid marriage, of the dignity which their reduced situation, and Mr Dudley's being obliged to take orders for a country living, had so much lessened. They at once despised the Percivals as people of mean family, and envied them as people of fortune. They were jealous of their being more respected than themselves, and while they affected to consider them as of no consequence, were continually seeking to lessen them in the opinion of the neighbourhood by scandalous and malicious reports.

Such a family as this was ill-calculated to console Kitty for the loss of the Wynnes, or to fill up by their society those occasionally irksome hours which in so retired a situation would sometimes occur for want of a companion. Her aunt was most excessively fond of her, and miserable if she saw her for a moment out of spirits. Yet she lived in such constant apprehension of her marrying imprudently if she were allowed the opportunity of choosing, and was so dissatisfied with her behaviour when she saw her with young men – for it was, from her natural disposition, remarkably open and unreserved – that though she frequently wished for her niece's sake that the neighbourhood were larger, and that she had used herself to mix more with it, yet the recollection of there being young men in almost every family in it, always conquered the wish.

The same fears that prevented Mrs Percival's joining much in the society of her neighbours led her equally to avoid inviting her relations to spend any time in her house – she had therefore constantly regretted the annual attempt of a distant relation to visit her at Chetwynde, as there was a young man in the family of whom she had heard many traits that alarmed her. This son was, however, now on his travels, and the repeated solicitations of Kitty, joined to a consciousness of having declined with too little ceremony the frequent overtures of her friends to be admitted, and a real wish to see them herself, easily prevailed on her to press with great earnestness the pleasure of a visit from them during the summer.

Mr and Mrs Stanley were accordingly to come, and Catharine, in having an object to look forward to, a something to expect that must inevitably relieve the dullness of a constant tête-à-tête with her aunt, was so delighted, and her spirits so elevated, that for the three or four days immediately preceding their arrival she could scarcely fix herself to any employment. In this point Mrs Percival always thought her defective, and frequently complained of a want of steadiness and perseverance in her occupations, which were by no means congenial to the eagerness of Kitty's disposition, and perhaps not often met with in any young person. The tediousness too of her aunt's conversation and the want of agreeable companions greatly increased this desire of change in her employments, for Kitty found herself much sooner tired of reading, working, or drawing in Mrs Percival's parlour than in her own arbour, where Mrs Percival for fear of its being damp never accompanied her.

As her aunt prided herself on the exact propriety and neatness with which everything in her family was conducted, and had no higher satisfaction than that of knowing her house to be always in complete order, as her fortune was good, and her establishment ample, few were the preparations necessary for the reception of her visitors. The day of their arrival so long expected, at length came, and the noise of the coach and four as it drove round the sweep was to Catharine a more interesting sound than the music of an Italian opera, which to most heroines is the height of enjoyment. Mr and Mrs Stanley were people of large fortune and high fashion. He was a Member of the House of Commons, and they were therefore most agreeably necessitated to reside half the year in town, where Miss Stanley had been attended by the most capital masters from the time of her being six years old to the last spring; which, comprehending a period of twelve years, had been dedicated to the acquirement of accomplishments which were now to be displayed and in a few years entirely neglected.

She was not inelegant in her appearance, rather handsome, and naturally not deficient in abilities; but those years which ought to have been spent in the attainment of useful knowledge and mental improvement, had been all bestowed in learning drawing, Italian and music, more especially the latter, and she now united to these accomplishments, an understanding unimproved by reading and a mind totally devoid either of taste or judgement. Her temper was by nature good, but unassisted by reflection, she had neither patience under disappointment, nor could sacrifice her own inclinations to promote the happiness of others. All her ideas were towards the elegance of her appearance, the fashion of her dress, and the admiration she wished them to excite. She professed a love of books without reading, was lively without wit, and generally good humoured without merit.

Such was Camilla Stanley; and Catharine, who was prejudiced by her appearance, and who from her solitary situation was ready to like anyone, though her understanding and judgement would not otherwise have been easily satisfied, felt almost convinced, when she saw her, that Miss Stanley would be the very companion she wanted, and in some degree make amends for the loss of Cecilia and Mary Wynne. She therefore attached herself to Camilla from the first day of her arrival, and from being the only young people in the house, they were by inclination constant companions. Kitty was herself a great reader, though perhaps not a very deep one, and felt therefore highly delighted to find that Miss Stanley was equally fond of it. Eager to know that their sentiments as to books were similar, she very soon began questioning her new acquaintance on the subject; but though she was well read in modern history herself, she chose rather to speak first of books of a lighter kind, of books universally read and admired.

'You have read Mrs Smith's novels,[3] I suppose?' said she to her companion.

'Oh! yes,' replied the other, 'and I am quite delighted with them. They are the sweetest things in the world –'

'And which do you prefer of them?'

'Oh! dear, I think there is no comparison between them – *Emmeline* is *so much* better than any of the others –'

'Many people think so, I know; but there does not appear so great a disproportion in their merits to *me*. Do you think it is better written?'

'Oh! I do not know anything about *that* – but it is better in *everything* –. Besides, *Ethelinde* is so long –'

'That is a very common objection, I believe,' said Kitty, 'but for my own part, if a book is well written, I always find it too short.'

'So do I, only I get tired of it before it is finished.'

'But did not you find the story of *Ethelinde* very interesting? And the descriptions of Grasmere, are not they beautiful?'

'Oh! I missed them all, because I was in such a hurry to know the end of it.' Then, from an easy transition, she added, 'We are going to the Lakes this autumn, and I am quite mad with joy; Sir Henry Devereux has promised to go with us, and that will make it so pleasant, you know –'

'I dare say it will; but I think it is a pity that Sir Henry's powers of pleasing were not reserved for an occasion where they might be more wanted. However I quite envy you the pleasure of such a scheme.'

'Oh! I am quite delighted with the thoughts of it; I can think of nothing else. I assure you I have done nothing for this last month but plan what clothes I should take with me, and I have at last determined to take very few indeed besides my travelling dress, and so I advise you to do whenever you go; for I intend in case we should fall in with any races, or stop at Matlock or Scarborough, to have some things made for the occasion.'

'You intend then to go into Yorkshire?'

'I believe not – indeed I know nothing of the route, for I never trouble myself about such things. I only know that we are to go from Derbyshire to Matlock and Scarborough, but to which of them first, I neither know nor care. I am in hopes of meeting some particular friends of mine at Scarborough – Augusta told me in her last letter that Sir Peter talked of going; but then you know that is so uncertain. I cannot bear Sir Peter, he is such a horrid creature –'

'He *is*, is he?' said Kitty, not knowing what else to say.

'Oh! he is quite shocking.'

Here the conversation was interrupted, and Kitty was left in a painful uncertainty as to the particulars of Sir Peter's character; she knew only that he was horrid and shocking, but why, and in what, yet remained to be discovered. She could scarcely resolve what to think of her new acquaintance; she appeared to be shamefully ignorant as to the geography of England, if she had understood her right, and equally devoid of taste and information. Kitty was, however, unwilling to decide hastily; she was at once desirous of doing Miss Stanley justice, and of having her own wishes in her answered; she determined therefore to suspend all judgement for some time.

After supper, the conversation turning on the state of affairs in the political world, Mrs Percival, who was firmly of the opinion that the whole race of mankind were degenerating, said that, for her part, everything she believed was going to rack and ruin, all order was destroyed over the face of the world, the House of Commons she heard did not break up sometimes till five in the morning, and depravity never was so general before; concluding with a wish that she might live to see the manners of the people in Queen Elizabeth's reign, restored again.

'Well, ma'am,' said her niece, 'but I hope you do not mean with the times to restore Queen Elizabeth herself.'

'Queen Elizabeth,' said Mrs Stanley, who never hazarded a remark on history that was not well founded, 'lived to a good old age, and was a very clever woman.'

'True, ma'am,' said Kitty. 'But I do not consider either of those circumstances as meritorious in herself, and they are very far from making me wish her return, for if she were to come again with the same abilities and the same good constitution she might do as much mischief and last as long as she did before.' Then, turning to Camilla who had been sitting very silent for some time, she added, 'What do *you* think of Elizabeth, Miss Stanley? I hope you will not defend her.'

'Oh! dear,' said Miss Stanley, 'I know nothing of politics, and cannot bear to hear them mentioned.' Kitty started at this repulse, but made no answer; that Miss Stanley must be ignorant of what she could not distinguish from politics she felt perfectly convinced. She retired to her own room, perplexed in her opinion about her new acquaintance, and fearful of her being very unlike Cecilia and Mary.

She arose the next morning to experience a fuller conviction of this, and every future day increased it. She found no variety in her conversation; she received no information from her but in fashions, and no amusement but in her performance on the harpsichord; and after repeated endeavours to find her what she wished, she was obliged to give up the attempt and to consider it as fruitless. There had occasionally appeared a something like humour in Camilla which had inspired her with hopes that she might at least have a natural genius, though not an improved one, but these sparklings of wit happened so seldom, and were so ill supported that she was at last convinced of their being merely accidental. All her stock of knowledge was exhausted in a very few days, and when Kitty had learnt from her how large their house in town was, when the fashionable amusements began, who were the celebrated beauties and who the best milliner, Camilla had nothing further to teach, except the characters of any of her acquaintance as they occurred in conversation, which was done with equal ease and brevity, by saying that the person was either the sweetest creature in the world, and one of whom she was dotingly fond, or horrid, shocking and not fit to be seen.

As Catharine was very desirous of gaining every possible information as to the characters of the Halifax family, and concluded that Miss Stanley must be acquainted with them, as she seemed to be so with every one of any consequence, she took an opportunity, as Camilla was one day enumerating all the people of rank that her mother visited, of asking her whether Lady Halifax were among the number.

'Oh! Thank you for reminding me of her; she is the sweetest woman in the world, and one of our most intimate acquaintance. I do not suppose there is a day passes during the six months that we are in town but what we see each other in the course of it. And I correspond with all the girls.'

'They *are* then a very pleasant family!' said Kitty. 'They ought to be so indeed, to allow of such frequent meetings, or all conversation must be at end.'

'Oh! dear, not at all,' said Miss Stanley, 'for sometimes we do not speak to each other for a month together. We meet perhaps only in public, and then you know we are often not able to get near enough; but in that case we always nod and smile.'

'Which does just as well –. But I was going to ask you whether you have ever seen a Miss Wynne with them?'

'I know who you mean perfectly – she wears a blue hat. I have frequently seen her in Brook Street, when I have been at Lady Halifax's balls – she gives one every month during the winter. But only think how good it is in her to take care of Miss Wynne, for she is a very distant relation, and so poor that, as Miss Halifax told me, her mother was obliged to find her in clothes. Is not it shameful?'

'That she should be so poor? It is indeed, with such wealthy connections as the family have.'

'Oh! no; I mean, was not it shameful in Mr Wynne to leave his children so distressed, when he had actually the living of

Chetwynde and two or three curacies, and only four children to provide for. What would he have done if he had had ten, as many people have?'

'He would have given them all a good education and have left them all equally poor.'

'Well I do think there never was so lucky a family. Sir George Fitzgibbon, you know, sent the eldest girl to India entirely at his own expense, where they say she is most nobly married and the happiest creature in the world. Lady Halifax, you see, has taken care of the youngest and treats her as if she were her daughter. She does not go out into public with her to be sure; but then she is always present when her ladyship gives her balls, and nothing can be kinder to her than Lady Halifax is; she would have taken her to Cheltenham last year if there had been room enough at the lodgings, and therefore I do not think that *she* can have anything to complain of. Then there are the two sons; one of them the Bishop of M** has got into the army as a lieutenant I suppose; and the other is extremely well off I know, for I have a notion that somebody puts him to school somewhere in Wales. Perhaps you knew them when they lived here?'

'Very well. We met as often as your family and the Halifaxes do in town, but as we seldom had any difficulty in getting near enough to speak, we seldom parted with merely a nod and a smile. They were indeed a most charming family, and I believe have scarcely their equals in the world; the neighbours we now have at the parsonage appear to more disadvantage in coming after them.'

'Oh! horrid wretches! I wonder you can endure them.'

'Why, what would you have one do?'

'Oh! Lord, if I were in your place, I should abuse them all day long.'

'So I do, but it does no good.'

'Well, I declare it is quite a pity that they should be suffered to live. I wish my father would propose knocking all their brains out some day or other when he is in the House. So abominably proud of their family! And I dare say after all, that there is nothing particular in it.'

'Why yes, I believe they *have* reason to value themselves on it, if anybody has; for you know he is Lord Amyatt's brother.'

'Oh! I know all that very well, but it is no reason for their being so horrid. I remember I met Miss Dudley last spring with Lady Amyatt at Ranelagh⁴, and she had such a frightful cap on that I have never been able to bear any of them since. And so you used to think the Wynnes very pleasant?'

'You speak as if their being so were doubtful! Pleasant! Oh! they were everything that could interest and attach. It is not in my power to do justice to their merits, though not to feel them, I think must be impossible. They have unfitted me for any society but their own!'

'Well, that is just what I think of the Miss Halifaxes; by the by, I must write to Caroline tomorrow, and I do not know what to say to her. The Barlows too are just such other sweet girls; but I wish Augusta's hair was not so dark. I cannot bear Sir Peter – horrid wretch! He is *always* laid up with the gout, which is exceedingly disagreeable to the family.'

'And perhaps not very pleasant to *himself*. But as to the Wynnes: do you really think them very fortunate?'

'Do I? Why, does not everybody? Miss Halifax and Caroline and Maria all say that they are the luckiest creatures in the world. So does Sir George Fitzgibbon and so do everybody.'

'That is, everybody who have themselves conferred an obligation on them. But do you call it lucky for a girl of genius and feeling to be sent in quest of a husband to Bengal, to be married there to a man of whose disposition she has no opportunity of judging till her judgement is of no use to her, who may be a tyrant, or a fool, or both, for what she knows to the contrary. Do you call *that* fortunate?'

'I know nothing of all that; I only know that it was extremely good in Sir George to fit her out and pay her passage, and that she would not have found many who would have done the same.'

'I wish she had not found *one*,' said Kitty, with great eagerness, 'she might then have remained in England and been happy.'

'Well, I cannot conceive the hardship of going out in a very agreeable manner with two or three sweet girls for companions, having a delightful voyage to Bengal or Barbados or wherever it is, and being married soon after one's arrival to a very charming man, immensely rich. I see no hardship in all that.'

'Your representation of the affair,' said Kitty, laughing, 'certainly gives a very different idea of it from mine. But supposing all this to be true; still, as it was by no means certain that she would be so fortunate either in her voyage, her companions, or her husband, in being obliged to run the risk of their proving very different, she undoubtedly experienced a great hardship. Besides, to a girl of any delicacy, the voyage in itself, since the object of it is so universally known, is a punishment that needs no other to make it very severe.'

'I do not see that at all. She is not the first girl who has gone to the East Indies for a husband, and I declare I should think it very good fun if I were as poor.'

'I believe you would think very differently *then*. But at least you will not defend her sister's situation! Dependent even for her clothes on the bounty of others, who of course do not pity her, as by your own account, they consider her as very fortunate.'

'You are extremely nice[5] upon my word; Lady Halifax is a delightful woman, and one of the sweetest-tempered creatures in the world; I am sure I have every reason to speak well of her, for we are under most amazing obligations to her. She has frequently chaperoned me when my mother has been indisposed, and last spring she lent me her own horse three times, which was a prodigious favour, for it is the most beautiful creature that ever was seen, and I am the only person she ever lent it to.

'And then,' continued she, 'the Miss Halifaxes are quite delightful. Maria is one of the cleverest girls that ever were known – draws in oils, and plays anything by sight. She promised me one of her drawings before I left town, but I entirely forgot to ask her for it. I would give anything to have one.'

'But was not it very odd,' said Kitty, 'that the bishop should send Charles Wynne to sea, when he must have had a much better chance of providing for him in the Church, which was the profession that Charles liked best, and the one for which his father had intended him? The Bishop I know had often promised Mr Wynne a living, and as he never gave him one, I think it was incumbent on him to transfer the promise to his son.'

'I believe you think he ought to have resigned his bishopric to him; you seem determined to be dissatisfied with everything that has been done for them.'

'Well,' said Kitty, 'this is a subject on which we shall never agree, and therefore it will be useless to continue it further, or to mention it again –'

She then left the room, and running out of the house was soon in her dear bower, where she could indulge in peace all her affectionate anger against the relations of the Wynnes, which was greatly heightened by finding from Camilla that they were in general considered as having acted particularly well by them. She amused herself for some time in abusing and hating them all with great spirit, and when this tribute to her regard for the Wynnes was paid, and the bower began to have its usual influence over her spirits, she contributed towards settling them by taking out a book, for she had always one about her, and reading.

She had been so employed for nearly an hour when Camilla came running towards her with great eagerness, and apparently great pleasure. 'Oh! my dear Catharine,' said she, half out of breath, 'I have such delightful news for you – but you shall guess what it is –. We are all the happiest creatures in the world; would you believe it, the Dudleys have sent us an invitation to a ball at their own house –. What charming people they are! I had no idea of there being so much sense in the whole family – I declare I quite dote upon them. And it happens so fortunately too, for I expect a new cap from town tomorrow which will just do for a ball – gold net – it will be a most angelic thing – everybody will be longing for the pattern –'

The expectation of a ball was indeed very agreeable intelligence to Kitty, who, fond of dancing and seldom able to enjoy it, had reason to feel even greater pleasure in it than her friend; for to *her*, it was now no novelty. Camilla's delight, however, was by no means inferior to Kitty's, and she rather expressed the most of the two. The cap came and every other preparation was soon completed; while these were in agitation the days passed gaily away, but when directions were no longer necessary, taste could no longer be displayed, and difficulties no longer overcome, the short period that intervened before the day of the ball hung heavily on their hands, and every hour was too long. The very few times that Kitty had ever enjoyed the amusement of dancing was an excuse for *her* impatience, and an apology for the idleness it occasioned to a mind naturally very active; but her friend without such a plea was infinitely worse than herself. She could do nothing but wander from the house to the garden, and from the garden to the avenue, wondering when Thursday would come, which she might easily have ascertained, and counting the hours as they passed, which served only to lengthen them.

They retired to their rooms in high spirits on Wednesday night, but Kitty awoke the next morning with a violent toothache. It was in vain that she endeavoured at first to deceive herself; her feelings were witnesses too acute of its reality; with as little success did she try to sleep it off, for the pain she suffered prevented her closing her eyes.

She then summoned her maid and, with the assistance of the housekeeper, every remedy that the receipt book or the head of the latter contained, was tried, but ineffectually; for though for a short time relieved by them, the pain still returned. She was now obliged to give up the endeavour, and to reconcile herself not only to the pain of a toothache, but to the loss of a ball; and though she had with so much eagerness looked forward to the day of its arrival, had received such pleasure in the necessary preparations, and promised herself so much delight in it, yet she was not so totally void of philosophy as many girls of her age might have been in her situation. She considered that there were misfortunes of a much greater magnitude than the loss of a ball experienced every day by some part of mortality, and that the time might come when she would herself look back with wonder and perhaps with envy on her having known no greater vexation. By such reflections as these, she soon reasoned herself into as much resignation and patience as the pain she suffered would allow of, which after all was the greatest misfortune of the two, and told the sad story when she entered the breakfast room with tolerable composure.

Mrs Percival – more grieved for her toothache than her disappointment, as she feared that it would not be possible to prevent her dancing with a *man* if she went – was eager to try everything that had already been applied to alleviate the pain, while at the same time she declared it was impossible for her to leave the house. Miss Stanley, who, joined to her concern for her friend, felt a mixture of dread lest her mother's proposal that they should all remain at home might be accepted, was very violent in her sorrow on the occasion, and though her apprehensions on the subject were soon quieted by Kitty's protesting that sooner than allow anyone to stay with her, she would herself go, she continued to lament it with such unceasing vehemence as at last drove Kitty to her own room. Her fears for herself being now entirely dissipated left her more than ever at leisure to pity and persecute her friend who, though safe when in her own room, was frequently removing from it to some other in hopes of being more free from pain, and then had no opportunity of escaping her.

'To be sure, there never was anything so shocking,' said Camilla. 'To come on such a day too! For one would not have minded it you know had it been at *any other* time. But it always is so. I never was at a ball in my life but what something happened to prevent somebody from going! I wish there were no such things as teeth in the world; they are nothing but plagues to one, and I dare say that people might easily invent something to eat with instead of them. Poor thing! What pain you are in! I declare it is quite shocking to look at you. But you won't have it out, will you! For heaven's sake don't, for there is nothing I dread so much. I declare I had rather undergo the greatest tortures in the world than have a tooth drawn. Well! how patiently you do bear it! How can you be so quiet! Lord, if I were in your place I should make such a fuss, there would be no bearing me. I should torment you to death.'

'So you do, as it is,' thought Kitty.

'For my own part, Catharine,' said Mrs Percival, 'I have not a doubt but that you caught this toothache by sitting so much in that arbour, for it is always damp. I know it has ruined your constitution entirely; and indeed I do not believe it has been of much service to mine. I sat down in it last May to rest myself, and I have never been quite well since. I shall order John to pull it all down, I assure you.'

'I know you will not do that, ma'am,' said Kitty, 'as you must be convinced how unhappy it would make me.'

'You talk very ridiculously, child; it is all whim and nonsense. Why cannot you fancy this room an arbour!'

'Had this room been built by Cecilia and Mary, I should have valued it equally, ma'am, for it is not merely the name of an arbour which charms me.'

'Why indeed, Mrs Percival,' said Mrs Stanley, 'I must think that Catharine's affection for her bower is the effect of a sensibility that does her credit. I love to see a friendship between young persons and always consider it as a sure mark of an amiable affectionate disposition. I have, from Camilla's infancy, taught her to think the same, and have taken great pains to introduce her to young people of her own age who were likely to be worthy of her regard. Nothing forms the taste more than sensible and elegant letters. Lady Halifax thinks just like me. Camilla corresponds with her daughters, and I believe I may venture to say that they are none of them *the worse* for it.'

These ideas were too modern to suit Mrs Percival who considered a correspondence between girls as productive of no good, and as the frequent origin of imprudence and error by the effect of pernicious advice and bad example. She could not therefore refrain from saying that, for her part, she had lived fifty years in the world without having ever had a correspondent, and did not find herself at all the less respectable for it.

Mrs Stanley could say nothing in answer to this, but her daughter, who was less governed by propriety, said in her thoughtless way, 'But who knows what you might have been, ma'am, if you *had* had a correspondent; perhaps it would have made you quite a different creature. I declare I would not be without those I have for all the world. It is the greatest delight of my life, and you cannot think how much their letters have formed my taste, as Mama says, for I hear from them generally every week.'

'You received a letter from Augusta Barlow today, did not you, my love,' said her mother. 'She writes remarkably well I know.'

'Oh! Yes, ma'am, the most delightful letter you ever heard of. She sends me a long account of the new Regency walking dress Lady Susan has given her, and it is so beautiful that I am quite dying with envy for it.'

'Well, I am prodigiously happy to hear such pleasing news of my young friend; I have a high regard for Augusta, and most sincerely partake in the general joy on the occasion. But does she say nothing else? It seemed to be a long letter – are they to be at Scarborough?'

'Oh! Lord, she never once mentions it, now I recollect it;

and I entirely forgot to ask her when I wrote last. She says nothing indeed except about the Regency.'

'She *must* write well,' thought Kitty, 'to make a long letter upon a bonnet and pelisse.' She then left the room, tired of listening to a conversation which, though it might have diverted her had she been well, served only to fatigue and depress her while in pain.

Happy was it for *her* when the hour of dressing came, for Camilla, satisfied with being surrounded by her mother and half the maids in the house, did not want her assistance, and was too agreeably employed to want her society. She remained therefore alone in the parlour, till joined by Mr Stanley and her aunt, who, however, after a few enquiries, allowed her to continue undisturbed, and began their usual conversation on politics. This was a subject on which they could never agree, for Mr Stanley, who considered himself as perfectly qualified, by his seat in the House, to decide on it without hesitation, resolutely maintained that the kingdom had not for ages been in so flourishing and prosperous a state, and Mrs Percival, with equal warmth, though perhaps less argument, as vehemently asserted that the whole nation would speedily be ruined, and everything, as she expressed herself, be at sixes and sevens.

It was not, however, unamusing to Kitty to listen to the dispute, especially as she began then to be more free from pain, and, without taking any share in it herself, she found it very entertaining to observe the eagerness with which they both defended their opinions, and could not help thinking that Mr Stanley would not feel more disappointed if her aunt's expectations were fulfilled than her aunt would be mortified by their failure.

After waiting a considerable time, Mrs Stanley and her

daughter appeared, and Camilla, in high spirits and perfect good humour with her own looks, was more violent than ever in her lamentations over her friend as she practised her Scotch steps about the room. At length they departed, and Kitty, better able to amuse herself than she had been the whole day before, wrote a long account of her misfortunes to Mary Wynne.

When her letter was concluded she had an opportunity of witnessing the truth of that assertion which says that sorrows are lightened by communication, for her toothache was then so much relieved that she began to entertain an idea of following her friends to Mr Dudley's. They had been gone an hour, and as everything relative to her dress was in complete readiness, she considered that in another hour, since there was so little a way to go, she might be there.

They were gone in Mr Stanley's carriage, and therefore she might follow in her aunt's. As the plan seemed so very easy to be executed, and promising so much pleasure, it was after a few minutes' deliberation finally adopted; and running upstairs, she rang in great haste for her maid. The bustle and hurry which then ensued for nearly an hour was at last happily concluded by her finding herself very well dressed and in high beauty. Anne was then dispatched in the same haste to order the carriage, while her mistress was putting on her gloves, and arranging the folds of her dress.

In a few minutes she heard the carriage drive up to the door, and though at first surprised at the expedition with which it had been got ready, she concluded after a little reflection that the men had received some hint of her intentions beforehand, and was hastening out of the room, when Anne came running into it in the greatest hurry and agitation, exclaiming:

'Lord, ma'am! Here's a gentleman in a chaise and four

ne, and I cannot for the life conceive who it is! I happened to be crossing the hall when the carriage drove up, and I knew nobody would be in the way to let him in but Tom, and he looks so awkward you know, ma'am, now his hair is just done up, that I was not willing the gentleman should see him, and so I went to the door myself. And he is one of the handsomest young men you would wish to see; I was almost ashamed of being seen in my apron, ma'am, but, however, he is vastly handsome and did not seem to mind it at all. And he asked me whether the family were at home; and so I said everybody was gone out but you, ma'am, for I would not deny you because I was sure you would like to see him. And then he asked me whether Mr and Mrs Stanley were not here, and so I said yes, and then –'

'Good Heavens!' said Kitty, 'what can all this mean? And who can it possibly be? Did you never see him before? And did not he tell you his name?'

'No, ma'am, he never said anything about it – so then I asked him to walk into the parlour, and he was prodigious agreeable, and –'

'Whoever he is,' said her mistress, 'he has made a great impression upon you, Nanny – but where did he come from? And what does he want here?'

'Oh! ma'am, I was going to tell you that I fancy his business is with you, for he asked me whether you were at leisure to see anybody, and desired I would give his compliments to you, and say he should be very happy to wait on you. However, I thought he had better not come up into your dressing room, especially as everything is in such a litter, so I told him if he would be so obliging as to stay in the parlour, I would run upstairs and tell you he was come, and I dared to say that you would wait upon *him*. Lord, ma'am, I'd lay anything that he is come to ask you to dance with him tonight, and has got his chaise ready to take you to Mr Dudley's.'

Kitty could not help laughing at this idea, and only wished it might be true, as it was very likely that she would be too late for any other partner.

'But what, in the name of wonder, can he have to say to me! Perhaps he is come to rob the house – he comes in style at least, and it will be some consolation for our losses to be robbed by a gentleman in a chaise and four. What livery has his servants?'

'Why that is the most wonderful thing about him, ma'am, for he has not a single servant with him, and came back with hack horses; but he is as handsome as a prince for all that, and has quite the look of one. Do, dear ma'am, go down, for I am sure you will be delighted with him –'

'Well, I believe I must go; but it is very odd! What can he have to say to me.' Then giving one look at herself in the glass, she walked with great impatience – though trembling all the while from not knowing what to expect – downstairs, and after pausing a moment at the door to gather courage for opening it, she resolutely entered the room. The stranger, whose appearance did not disgrace the account she had received of it from her maid, rose up on her entrance, and laying aside the newspaper he had been reading, advanced towards her with an air of the most perfect ease and vivacity, and said to her:

'It is certainly a very awkward circumstance to be thus obliged to introduce myself, but I trust that the necessity of the case will plead my excuse, and prevent your being prejudiced by it against me –. *Your* name, I need not ask, ma'am. Miss Percival is too well known to me by description to need any information of that.' Kitty, who had been expecting him to tell his own name instead of hers, and who from having been little in company, and never before in such a situation, felt herself unable to ask it, though she had been planning her speech all the way downstairs, was so confused and distressed by this unexpected address that she could only return a slight curtsy to it, and accepted the chair he reached her, without knowing what she did.

The gentleman then continued. 'You are, I dare say, surprised to see me returned from France so soon, and nothing indeed but business could have brought me to England; a very melancholy affair has now occasioned it, and I was unwilling to leave it without paying my respects to the family in Devonshire whom I have so long wished to be acquainted with –'

Kitty, who felt much more surprised at his supposing her to *be* so than at seeing a person in England whose having ever left it was perfectly unknown to her, still continued silent from wonder and perplexity, and her visitor still continued to talk.

'You will suppose, madam, that I was not the *less* desirous of waiting on you, from your having Mr and Mrs Stanley with you. I hope they are well? And Mrs Percival, how does *she* do?' Then, without waiting for an answer, he gaily added, 'But my dear Miss Percival, you are going out I am sure, and I am detaining you from your appointment. How can I ever expect to be forgiven for such injustice! Yet how can I, so circumstanced, forbear to offend! You seem dressed for a ball! But this is the land of gaiety, I know; I have for many years been desirous of visiting it. You have dances, I suppose, at least every week – but where are the rest of your party gone, and what kind angel, in compassion to me, has excluded *you* from it?'

'Perhaps, sir,' said Kitty, extremely confused by his manner of speaking to her, and highly displeased with the freedom of his conversation towards one who had never seen him before and did not *now* know his name, 'perhaps, sir, you are acquainted with Mr and Mrs Stanley; and your business may be with *them*?'

'You do me too much honour, ma'am,' replied he laughing, 'in supposing me to be acquainted with Mr and Mrs Stanley; I merely know them by sight; very distant relations; only my father and mother. Nothing more I assure you.'

'Gracious Heaven! said Kitty, 'are *you* Mr Stanley, then? – I beg a thousand pardons – though really upon recollection I do not know for what – for you never told me your name –'

'I beg your pardon – I made a very fine speech when you entered the room, all about introducing myself; I assure you it was very great for *me*.'

'The speech had certainly great merit,' said Kitty smiling; 'I thought so at the time; but since you never mentioned your name in it, as an *introductory* one it might have been better.'

There was such an air of good humour and gaiety in Stanley that Kitty, though perhaps not authorised to address him with so much familiarity on so short an acquaintance, could not forbear indulging the natural unreserve and vivacity of her own disposition in speaking to him as he spoke to her. She was intimately acquainted too with his family who were her relations, and she chose to consider herself entitled by the connection to forget how little a while they had known each other.

'Mr and Mrs Stanley and your sister are extremely well,' said she, 'and will, I dare say, be very much surprised to see you – but I am sorry to hear that your return to England has been occasioned by an unpleasant circumstance.'

'Oh, don't talk of it,' said he, 'it is a most confounded shocking affair, and makes me miserable to think of it. But where are my father and mother, and your aunt gone! Oh! Do you know that I met the prettiest little waiting maid in the world when I came here; she let me into the house; I took her for you at first.'

'You did me a great deal of honour, and give me more credit for good nature than I deserve, for I *never* go to the door when anyone comes.'

'Nay, do not be angry; I mean no offence. But tell me, where are you going to so smart? Your carriage is just coming round.'

'I am going to a dance at a neighbour's, where your family and my aunt are already gone.'

'Gone, without you! What's the meaning of *that*? But I suppose you are like myself, rather long in dressing.'

'I must have been so indeed, if that were the case, for they have been gone nearly these two hours; the reason, however, was not what you suppose – I was prevented going by a pain –'

'By a pain!' interrupted Stanley, 'Oh! heavens, that is dreadful indeed! No matter where the pain was. But my dear Miss Percival, what do you say to my accompanying you! And suppose you were to dance with me too? *I* think it would be very pleasant.'

'I can have no objection to either, I am sure,' said Kitty, laughing to find how near the truth her maid's conjecture had been; 'on the contrary I shall be highly honoured by both, and I can answer for your being extremely welcome to the family who give the ball.'

'Oh! hang them; who cares for that; they cannot turn me out of the house. But I am afraid I shall cut a sad figure among all your Devonshire beaux in this dusty travelling apparel, and I have not wherewithal to change it. You can procure me some powder perhaps, and I must get a pair of shoes from one of the men, for I was in such a devil of a hurry to leave Lyons that I had not time to have anything packed up but some linen.'

Kitty very readily undertook to procure for him everything he wanted, and telling the footman to show him into Mr Stanley's dressing room, gave Nanny orders to send in some powder and pomatum, which orders Nanny chose to execute in person. As Stanley's preparations in dressing were confined to such very trifling articles, Kitty of course expected him in about ten minutes; but she found that it had not been merely a boast of vanity in saying that he was dilatory in that respect, as he kept her waiting for him above half an hour, so that the clock had struck ten before he entered the room and the rest of the party had gone by eight.

'Well,' said he as he came in, 'have not I been very quick! I never hurried so much in my life before.'

'In that case you certainly have,' replied Kitty, 'for all merit you know is comparative.'

'Oh! I knew you would be delighted with me for making so much haste. But come, the carriage is ready; so, do not keep me waiting.' And so saying he took her by the hand, and led her out of the room.

'Why, my dear cousin,' said he when they were seated, 'this will be a most agreeable surprise to everybody to see you enter the room with such a smart young fellow as I am – I hope your aunt won't be alarmed.'

'To tell you the truth,' replied Kitty, 'I think the best way to prevent it will be to send for her or your mother before we go into the room, especially as you are a perfect stranger, and must of course be introduced to Mr and Mrs Dudley –'

'Oh! nonsense,' said he; 'I did not expect *you* to stand upon such ceremony; our acquaintance with each other renders all such prudery ridiculous; besides, if we go in together, we shall be the whole talk of the country –'

'To *me*,' replied Kitty, 'that would certainly be a most powerful inducement; but I scarcely know whether my aunt would consider it as such. Women at her time of life have odd ideas of propriety, you know.'

'Which is the very thing that you ought to break them of; and why should you object to entering a room with me where all our relations are, when you have done me the honour to admit me without any chaperone into your carriage? Do not you think your aunt will be as much offended with you for one, as for the other of these mighty crimes?'

'Why really,' said Catharine, 'I do not know but that she may; however, it is no reason that I should offend against decorum a second time, because I have already done it once.'

'On the contrary, that is the very reason which makes it impossible for you to prevent it, since you cannot offend for the *first time* again.'

'You are very ridiculous,' said she, laughing, 'but I am afraid your arguments divert me too much to convince me.'

'At least they will convince you that I am very agreeable, which, after all, is the happiest conviction for me, and as to the affair of propriety we will let that rest till we arrive at our journey's end. This is a monthly ball I suppose. Nothing but dancing here –'

'I thought I had told you that it was given by a Mr and Mrs Dudley –'

'Oh! aye so you did; but why should not Mr Dudley give one every month! By the by, who *is* that man? Everybody gives balls now, I think; I believe I must give one myself soon. Well, but how do you like my father and mother? And poor little Camilla too, has not she plagued you to death with the Halifaxes?' Here the carriage fortunately stopped at Mr Dudley's, and Stanley was too much engaged in handing her out of it to wait for an answer, or to remember that what he had said required one.

They entered the small vestibule which Mr Dudley had raised to the dignity of a hall, and Kitty immediately desired the footman, who was leading the way upstairs, to inform either Mrs Percival or Mrs Stanley of her arrival, and beg them to come to her. But Stanley, unused to any contradiction, and impatient to be amongst them, would neither allow her to wait, or listen to what she said, and forcibly seizing her arm within his, overpowered her voice with the rapidity of his own, and Kitty, half angry and half laughing, was obliged to go with him upstairs, and could even with difficulty prevail on him to relinquish her hand before they entered the room.

Mrs Percival was at that very moment engaged in conversation with a lady at the upper end of the room, to whom she had been giving a long account of her niece's unlucky disappointment, and the dreadful pain that she had with so much fortitude endured the whole day –

'I left her, however,' said she, 'thank heaven! a little better, and I hope she has been able to amuse herself with a book, poor thing! for she must otherwise be very dull. She is probably in bed by this time, which, while she is so poorly, is the best place for her, you know, ma'am.'

The lady was going to give her assent to this opinion, when the noise of voices on the stairs, and the footman's opening the door as if for the entrance of company, attracted the attention of everybody in the room; and as it was in one of those intervals between the dances when everyone seemed glad to sit down, Mrs Percival had a most unfortunate opportunity of seeing her niece, whom she had supposed in bed, or amusing herself as the height of gaiety with a book, enter the room most elegantly dressed, with a smile on her countenance, and a glow of mingled cheerfulness and confusion on her cheeks, attended by a young man uncommonly handsome, and who without any of her confusion, appeared to have all her vivacity.

Mrs Percival, colouring with anger and astonishment, rose from her seat, and Kitty walked eagerly towards her, impatient to account for what she saw appeared wonderful to everybody, and extremely offensive to *her*, while Camilla, on seeing her brother, ran instantly towards him, and very soon explained who he was by her words and actions. Mr Stanley, who so fondly doted on his son that the pleasure of seeing him again after an absence of three months prevented his feeling for the time any anger against him for returning to England without his knowledge, received him with equal surprise and delight; and soon comprehending the cause of his journey, forbore any further conversation with him, as he was eager to see his mother, and it was necessary that he should be introduced to Mr Dudley's family.

This introduction, to anyone but Stanley, would have been highly unpleasant, for they considered their dignity injured by his coming uninvited to their house, and received him with more than their usual haughtiness: but Stanley, who with a vivacity of temper seldom subdued, and a contempt of censure not to be overcome, possessed an opinion of his own consequence, and a perseverance in his own schemes which were not to be damped by the conduct of others, appeared not to perceive it. The civilities therefore which they coldly offered, he received with a gaiety and ease peculiar to himself, and then attended by his father and sister walked into another room where his mother was playing at cards, to experience another meeting, and undergo a repetition of pleasure, surprise and explanations.

While these were passing, Camilla, eager to communicate

all she felt to someone who would attend to her, returned to Catharine, and seating herself by her, immediately began.

'Well, did you ever know anything so delightful as this! But it always is so; I never go to a ball in my life but what something or other happens unexpectedly that is quite charming!'

'A ball,' replied Kitty, 'seems to be a most eventful thing to you –'

'Oh! Lord, it is indeed – but only think of my brother's returning so suddenly – and how shocking a thing it is that has brought him over! I never heard anything so dreadful –!'

'What is it, pray, that has occasioned his leaving France! I am sorry to find that it is a melancholy event.'

'Oh! it is beyond anything you can conceive! His favourite hunter, who was turned out in the park on his going abroad, somehow or other fell ill – no, I believe it was an accident; but however it was something or other, or else it was something else, and so they sent an express immediately to Lyons where my brother was, for they knew that he valued this mare more than anything else in the world besides; and so my brother set off directly for England, and without packing up another coat; I am quite angry with him about it; it was so shocking, you know, to come away without a change of clothes –'

'Why indeed,' said Kitty, 'it seems to have been a very shocking affair from beginning to end.'

'Oh! it is beyond anything you can conceive! I would rather have had *anything* happen than that he should have lost that mare.'

'Except his coming away without another coat.'

'Oh! yes, that has vexed me more than you can imagine. – Well, and so Edward got to Brampton just as the poor thing was dead; but as he could not bear to remain there *then*, he came off directly to Chetwynde on purpose to see us. I hope he may not go abroad again.'

'Do you think he will not?'

'Oh! dear, to be sure he must, but I wish he may not with all my heart –. You cannot think how fond I am of him! By the by are not you in love with him yourself?'

'To be sure I am,' replied Kitty, laughing, 'I am in love with every handsome man I see.'

'That is just like me – *I* am always in love with every handsome man in the world.'

'There you outdo me,' replied Catharine, 'for I am only in love with those I *do* see.'

Mrs Percival, who was sitting on the other side of her, and who began now to distinguish the words *love* and *handsome man*, turned hastily towards them and said, 'What are you talking of, Catharine?'

To which Catharine immediately answered with the simple artifice of a child, 'Nothing, ma'am.' She had already received a very severe lecture from her aunt on the imprudence of her behaviour during the whole evening. She blamed her for coming to the ball, for coming in the same carriage with Edward Stanley, and still more for entering the room with him. For the last-mentioned offence Catharine knew not what apology to give, and though she longed in answer to the second to say that she had not thought it would be civil to make Mr Stanley *walk*, she dared not so to trifle with her aunt, who would have been but the more offended by it. The first accusation, however, she considered as very unreasonable, as she thought herself perfectly justified in coming.

This conversation continued till Edward Stanley, entering the room, came instantly towards her, and telling her that everyone waited for *her* to begin the next dance, led her to the top of the room, for Kitty, impatient to escape from so unpleasant a companion, without the least hesitation, or one civil scruple at being so distinguished, immediately gave him her hand, and joyfully left her seat. This conduct, however, was highly resented by several young ladies present, and among the rest by Miss Stanley, whose regard for her brother, though *excessive*, and whose affection for Kitty, though *prodigious*, were not proof against such an injury to her importance and her peace.

Edward had, however, only consulted his own inclinations in desiring Miss Percival to begin the dance, nor had he any reason to know that it was either wished or expected by anyone else in the party. As an heiress she was certainly of consequence, but her birth gave her no other claim to it, for her father had been a merchant. It was this very circumstance which rendered this unfortunate affair so offensive to Camilla, for though she would sometimes boast, in the pride of her heart and her eagerness to be admired, that she did not know who her grandfather had been and was as ignorant of everything relative to genealogy as to astronomy (and, she might have added, geography), yet she was really proud of her family and connections, and easily offended if they were treated with neglect.

'I should not have minded it,' said she to her mother, 'if she had been *anybody* else's daughter; but to see her pretend to be above *me*, when her father was only a tradesman, is too bad! It is such an affront to our whole family! I declare I think Papa ought to interfere in it, but he never cares about anything but politics. If I were Mr Pitt or the Lord Chancellor,[6] he would take care I should not be insulted, but he never thinks about *me*; and it is so provoking that *Edward* should let her stand there. I wish with all my heart that he had never come to

England! I hope she may fall down and break her neck or sprain her ankle.'

Mrs Stanley perfectly agreed with her daughter concerning the affair, and though with less violence, expressed almost equal resentment at the indignity.

Kitty, in the meantime, remained insensible of having given anyone offence, and therefore unable either to offer an apology, or make a reparation; her whole attention was occupied by the happiness she enjoyed in dancing with the most elegant young man in the room, and everyone else was equally unregarded. The evening indeed to *her* passed off delightfully; he was her partner during the greatest part of it, and the united attractions that he possessed of person, address and vivacity, had easily gained that preference from Kitty which they seldom fail of obtaining from everyone. She was too happy to care either for her aunt's ill humour, which she could not help remarking, or for the alteration in Camilla's behaviour, which forced itself at last on her observations. Her spirits were elevated above the influence of displeasure in anyone, and she was equally indifferent as to the cause of Camilla's or the continuance of her aunt's.

Though Mr Stanley could never be really offended by any imprudence or folly in his son that had given him the pleasure of seeing him, he was yet perfectly convinced that Edward ought not to remain in England, and was resolved to hasten his leaving it as soon as possible. But when he talked to Edward about it, he found him much less disposed towards returning to France than to accompany them in their projected tour, which, he assured his father, would be infinitely more pleasant to him; and that as to the affair of travelling he considered it of no importance, and what might be pursued at any little odd time when he had nothing better to do. He advanced these objections in a manner which plainly showed that he had scarcely a doubt of their being complied with, and appeared to consider his father's arguments in opposition to them as merely given with a view to keep up his authority, and such as he should find little difficulty in combating. He concluded at last by saying, as the chaise in which they returned together from Mr Dudley's reached Mrs Percival's:

'Well sir, we will settle this point some other time, and fortunately it is of so little consequence that an immediate discussion of it is unnecessary.' He then got out of the chaise and entered the house without waiting for his father's reply.

It was not till their return that Kitty could account for that coldness in Camilla's behaviour to her, which had been so pointed as to render it impossible to be entirely unnoticed. When, however, they were seated in the coach with the two other ladies, Miss Stanley's indignation was no longer to be suppressed from breaking out into words, and found the following vent.

'Well, I must say *this*, that I never was at a stupider ball in my life! But it always is so; I am always disappointed in them for some reason or other. I wish there were no such things.'

'I am sorry, Miss Stanley,' said Mrs Percival, drawing herself up, 'that you have not been amused; everything was meant for the best I am sure, and it is a poor encouragement for your mama to take you to another if you are so hard to be satisfied.'

'I do not know what you mean, ma'am, about Mama's *taking* me to another. You know I am come out.'

'Oh! dear Mrs Percival,' said Mrs Stanley, 'you must not believe everything that my lively Camilla says, for her spirits are prodigiously high sometimes, and she frequently speaks without thinking. I am sure it is impossible for *anyone* to have been at a more elegant or agreeable dance, and so she wishes to express herself, I am certain.'

'To be sure I do,' said Camilla very sulkily, 'only I must say that it is not very pleasant to have anybody behave so rude to one as to be quite shocking! I am sure I am not at all offended, and should not care if all the world were to stand above me, but still it is extremely abominable, and what I cannot put up with. It is not that I mind it in the least, for I had just as soon stand at the bottom as at the top all night long, if it was not so very disagreeable. But to have a person come in the middle of the evening and take everybody's place is what I am not used to, and though I do not care a pin about it myself, I assure you I shall not easily forgive or forget it.'

This speech, which perfectly explained the whole affair to Kitty, was shortly followed on her side by a very submissive apology, for she had too much good sense to be proud of her family, and too much good nature to live at variance with anyone. The excuses she made were delivered with so much real concern for the offence, and such unaffected sweetness that it was almost impossible for Camilla to retain that anger which had occasioned them. She felt, indeed, most highly gratified to find that no insult had been intended and that Catharine was very far from forgetting the difference in their birth for which she could *now* only pity her; and her good humour being restored with the same ease in which it had been affected, she spoke with the highest delight of the evening, and declared that she had never before been at so pleasant a ball.

The same endeavours that had procured the forgiveness of Miss Stanley ensured to her the cordiality of her mother, and nothing was wanting but Mrs Percival's good humour to render the happiness of the others complete; but she, offended with Camilla for her affected superiority, still more so with her brother for coming to Chetwynde, and dissatisfied with the whole evening, continued silent and gloomy and was a restraint on the vivacity of her companions.

She eagerly seized the very first opportunity which the next morning offered to her of speaking to Mr Stanley on the subject of his son's return, and after having expressed her opinion of its being a very silly affair that he came at all, concluded with desiring him to inform Mr Edward Stanley that it was a rule with her never to admit a young man into her house as a visitor for any length of time.

'I do not speak, sir,' she continued, 'out of any disrespect to you, but I could not answer it to myself to allow of his stay; there is no knowing what might be the consequence of it if he were to continue here, for girls nowadays will always give a handsome young man the preference before any other, though for why I never could discover, for what, after all, is youth and beauty! It is but a poor substitute for real worth and merit. Believe me, cousin, that whatever people may say to the contrary, there is certainly nothing like virtue for making us what we ought to be, and as to a young man's being young and handsome and having an agreeable person, it is nothing at all to the purpose for he had much better be respectable. I always *did* think so, and I always *shall*, and therefore you will oblige me very much by desiring your son to leave Chetwynde, or I cannot be answerable for what may happen between him and my niece. You will be surprised to hear *me* say it,' she continued, lowering her voice, 'but truth will out, and I must own that Kitty is one of the most impudent girls that ever existed. I assure you, sir, that I have seen her sit and laugh and whisper with a young man whom she has not seen above half a dozen times. Her behaviour indeed is scandalous, and therefore I beg you will send your son away immediately, or everything will be at sixes and sevens.'

Mr Stanley, who from one part of her speech had scarcely known to what length her insinuations of Kitty's impudence were meant to extend, now endeavoured to quiet her fears on the occasion by assuring her that on every account he meant to allow only of his son's continuing that day with them, and that she might depend on his being more earnest in the affair from a wish of obliging her. He added also that he knew Edward to be very desirous himself of returning to France, as he wisely considered all time lost that did not forward the plans in which he was at present engaged – though he was but too well convinced of the contrary himself.

His assurance in some degree quieted Mrs Percival, and left her tolerably relieved of her cares and alarms, and better disposed to behave with civility towards his son during the short remainder of his stay at Chetwynde. Mr Stanley went immediately to Edward, to whom he repeated the conversation that had passed between Mrs Percival and himself, and strongly pointed out the necessity of his leaving Chetwynde the next day, since his word was already engaged for it. His son, however, appeared struck only by the ridiculous apprehensions of Mrs Percival; and highly delighted at having occasioned them himself, seemed engrossed alone in thinking how he might increase them, without attending to any other part of his father's conversation. Mr Stanley could get no determinate answer from him, and though he still hoped for the best, they parted almost in anger on his side.

His son, though by no means disposed to marry, or any otherwise attached to Miss Percival than as a good-natured lively girl who seemed pleased with him, took infinite pleasure in alarming the jealous fears of her aunt by his attentions to her, without considering what effect they might have on the lady herself. He would always sit by her when she was in the room, appear dissatisfied if she left it, and was the first to enquire whether she meant soon to return. He was delighted with her drawings, and enchanted with her performance on the harpsichord; everything that she said appeared to interest him; his conversation was addressed to her alone, and she seemed to be the sole object of his attention.

That such efforts should succeed with one so tremblingly alive to every alarm of the kind as Mrs Percival, is by no means unnatural, and that they should have equal influence with her niece whose imagination was lively, and whose disposition romantic, who was already extremely pleased with him, and of course desirous that he might be so with her, is as little to be wondered at. Every moment, as it added to the conviction of his liking her, made him still more pleasing, and strengthened in her mind a wish of knowing him better.

As for Mrs Percival, she was in tortures the whole day. Nothing that she had ever felt before on a similar occasion was to be compared to the sensations which then distracted her; her fears had never been so strongly, or indeed so reasonably, excited. Her dislike of Stanley, her anger at her niece, her impatience to have them separated, conquered every idea of propriety and good breeding, and though he had never mentioned any intention of leaving them the next day, she could not help asking him after dinner, in her eagerness to have him gone, at what time he meant to set out.

'Oh! ma'am,' replied he, 'if I am off by twelve at night, you may think yourself lucky; and if I am not, you can only blame yourself for having left so much as the *hour* of my departure to my own disposal.'

Mrs Percival coloured very highly at this speech, and without addressing herself to anyone in particular, immediately began a long harangue on the shocking behaviour of modern young men, and the wonderful alteration that had taken place in them since her time, which she illustrated with many instructive anecdotes of the decorum and modesty which had marked the characters of those whom she had known when she had been young. This, however, did not prevent his walking in the garden with her niece, without any other companion, for nearly an hour in the course of the evening. They had left the room for that purpose with Camilla at a time when Mrs Percival had been out of it, nor was it for some time after her return to it that she could discover where they were.

Camilla had taken two or three turns with them in the walk which led to the arbour, but soon growing tired of listening to a conversation in which she was seldom invited to join, and from its turning occasionally on books, very little able to do it, she left them together in the arbour to wander alone to some other part of the garden, to eat the fruit, and examine Mrs Percival's greenhouse. Her absence was so far from being regretted that it was scarcely noticed by them, and they continued conversing together on almost every subject – for Stanley seldom dwelt long on any, and had something to say on all – till they were interrupted by her aunt.

Kitty was, by this time, perfectly convinced that both in natural abilities and acquired information, Edward Stanley was infinitely superior to his sister. Her desire of knowing that he was so had induced her to take every opportunity of turning the conversation on history and they were very soon engaged in a historical dispute, for which no one was more calculated than Stanley, who was so far from being really of any party that he had scarcely a fixed opinion on the subject. He could therefore always take either side, and always argue with temper. In his indifference on all such topics he was very unlike his companion whose judgement, being guided by her feelings which were eager and warm, was easily decided, and though it was not always infallible, she defended it with a spirit and enthusiasm which marked her own reliance on it.

They had continued therefore for sometime conversing in this manner on the character of Richard III, which he was warmly defending, when he suddenly seized hold of her hand, and exclaiming with great emotion, 'Upon my honour, you are entirely mistaken,' pressed it passionately to his lips, and ran out of the arbour. Astonished at this behaviour, for which she was wholly unable to account, she continued for a few moments motionless on the seat where he had left her, and was then on the point of following him up the narrow walk through which he had passed, when on looking up the one that lay immediately before the arbour, she saw her aunt walking towards her with more than her usual quickness. This explained at once the reason for his leaving her, but his leaving her in such manner was rendered still more inexplicable by it. She felt a considerable degree of confusion at having been seen by her in such a place with Edward, and at having that part of his conduct for which she could not herself account witnessed by one to whom all gallantry was odious. She remained therefore confused, distressed and irresolute, and suffered her aunt to approach her, without leaving the arbour.

Mrs Percival's looks were by no means calculated to animate the spirits of her niece, who in silence awaited her accusation, and in silence meditated her defence. After a few moments' suspense, for Mrs Percival was too much fatigued to speak immediately, she began with great anger and asperity the following harangue.

'Well; *this* is beyond anything I could have supposed. *Profligate* as I *knew* you to be, I was not prepared for such a sight. This is beyond anything you ever did *before*; beyond anything I ever heard of in my life! Such impudence I never witnessed before in such a girl! And this is the reward for all the cares I have taken in your education; for all my troubles and anxieties; and Heaven knows how many they have been! All I wished for was to breed you up virtuously; I never wanted you to play upon the harpsichord, or draw better than anyone else; but I had hoped to see you respectable and good; to see you able and willing to give an example of modesty and virtue to the young people hereabouts. I bought you Blair's *Sermons*, and *Coelebs in Search of a Wife*,[7] I gave you the key to my own library, and borrowed a great many good books of my neighbours for you, all to this purpose. But I might have spared myself the trouble – Oh! Catharine, you are an abandoned creature, and I do not know what will become of you.

'I am glad, however,' she continued, softening into some degree of mildness, 'to see that you have some shame for what you have done, and if you are really sorry for it, and your future life is a life of penitence and reformation, perhaps you may be forgiven. But I plainly see that everything is going to sixes and sevens and all order will soon be at an end throughout the kingdom.'

'Not however, ma'am, the sooner, I hope, from any conduct of mine,' said Catharine, in a tone of great humility, 'for upon my honour I have done nothing this evening that can contribute to overthrow the establishment of the kingdom.'

'You are mistaken, child,' replied she; 'the welfare of every nation depends upon the virtue of its individuals, and anyone who offends in so gross a manner against decorum and propriety is certainly hastening its ruin. You have been giving a bad example to the world, and the world is but too well disposed to receive such.'

'Pardon me, madam,' said her niece; 'but I *can* have given an example only to *you*, for you alone have seen the offence. Upon my word, however, there is no danger to fear from what I have done; Mr Stanley's behaviour has given me as much surprise as it has done to you, and I can only suppose that it was the effect of his high spirits, authorised in his opinion by our relationship. But do you consider, madam, that it is growing very late! Indeed you had better return to the house.' This speech, as she well knew, would be unanswerable with her aunt, who instantly rose and hurried away under so many apprehensions for her own health as banished for the time all anxiety about her niece, who walked quietly by her side, revolving within her own mind the occurrence that had given her aunt so much alarm.

'I am astonished at my own imprudence,' said Mrs Percival. 'How could I be so forgetful as to sit down out of doors at such a time of night! I shall certainly have a return of my rheumatism after it – I begin to feel very chill already. I must have caught a dreadful cold by this time – I am sure of being lain up all the winter after it –'

Then, reckoning with her fingers, 'Let me see; this is July; the cold weather will soon be coming in – August – September – October – November – December – January – February – March – April – very likely I may not be tolerable again before May. I must and will have that arbour pulled down – it will be the death of me; who knows *now*, but what I may never recover – such things *have* happened. My particular friend Miss Sarah Hutchinson's death was occasioned by nothing more – she stayed out late one evening in April and got wet through for it rained very hard, and never changed her clothes when she came home. It is unknown how many people have died in consequence of catching cold! I do not believe there is a disorder in the world except the smallpox which does not spring from it.'

It was in vain that Kitty endeavoured to convince her that her fears on the occasion were groundless; that it was not yet late enough to catch cold, and that even if it were, she might hope to escape any other complaint, and to recover in less than ten months. Mrs Percival only replied that she hoped she knew more of ill health than to be convinced in such a point by a girl who had always been perfectly well, and hurried upstairs leaving Kitty to make her apologies to Mr and Mrs Stanley for going to bed. Though Mrs Percival seemed perfectly satisfied with the goodness of the apology herself, yet Kitty felt somewhat embarrassed to find that the only one she could offer to their visitors was that her aunt had perhaps caught cold, for Mrs Percival charged her to make light of it, for fear of alarming them.

Mr and Mrs Stanley, however, who well knew that their cousin was easily terrified on that score, received the account of it with very little surprise, and all proper concern.

Edward and his sister soon came in, and Kitty had no difficulty in gaining an explanation of his conduct from him, for he was too warm on the subject himself, and too eager to learn its success to refrain from making immediate enquiries about it; and she could not help feeling both surprised and offended at the ease and indifference with which he owned that all his intentions had been to frighten her aunt by pretending an affection for her, a design so very incompatible with that partiality which she had at one time been almost convinced of his feeling for her.

It is true that she had not yet seen enough of him to be actually in love with him, yet she felt greatly disappointed that so handsome, so elegant, so lively a young man should be so perfectly free from any such sentiment as to make it his principal sport. There was a novelty in his character which to *her* was extremely pleasing; his person was uncommonly fine, his spirits and vivacity suited to her own, and his manners at once so animated and insinuating that she thought it must be impossible for him to be otherwise than amiable, and was ready to give him credit for being perfectly so. He knew the powers of them himself; to them he had often been indebted for his father's forgiveness of faults which, had he been awkward and inelegant, would have appeared very serious; to them, even more than to his person or his fortune, he owed the regard which almost everyone was disposed to feel for him, and which young women in particular were inclined to entertain. Their influence was acknowledged on the present occasion by Kitty, whose anger they entirely dispelled, and whose cheerfulness they had power not only to restore, but to raise.

The evening passed off as agreeably as the one that had preceded it; they continued talking to each other during the chief part of it, and such was the power of his address, and the brilliancy of his eyes, that when they parted for the night, though Catharine had but a few hours before totally given up the idea, yet she felt almost convinced again that he was really in love with her. She reflected on their past conversation, and though it had been on various and indifferent subjects, and she could not exactly recollect any speech on his side expressive of such a partiality, she was still, however, nearly certain of its being so. But fearful of being vain enough to suppose such a thing without sufficient reason, she resolved to suspend her final determination on it till the next day, and more especially till their parting, which she thought would infallibly explain his regard, if any he had.

The more she had seen of him, the more inclined was she to like him, and the more desirous that he should like *her*. She was convinced of his being naturally very clever and very well disposed, and that his thoughtlessness and negligence – which though they appeared to *her* as very becoming in *him*, she was aware would by many people be considered as defects in his character – merely proceeded from a vivacity always pleasing in young men, and were far from testifying a weak or vacant understanding.

Having settled this point within herself, and being perfectly convinced by her own arguments of its truth, she went to bed in high spirits, determined to study his character and watch his behaviour still more the next day.

She got up with the same good resolutions and would probably have put them in execution, had not Anne informed her as soon as she entered the room that Mr Edward Stanley was already gone. At first she refused to credit the information, but when her maid assured her that he had ordered a carriage the evening before to be there at seven o'clock in the morning, and that she herself had actually seen him depart in it a little after eight, she could no longer deny her belief to it.

'And this,' thought she to herself, blushing with anger at her own folly, 'this is the affection for me of which I was so certain. Oh! what a silly thing is woman! How vain, how unreasonable! To suppose that a young man would be seriously attached in the course of four and twenty hours to a girl who has nothing to recommend her but a good pair of eyes! And he is really gone! Gone perhaps without bestowing a thought on me! Oh! why was not I up by eight o'clock! But it is a proper punishment for my laziness and folly, and I am heartily glad of it. I deserve it all, and ten times more for such insufferable vanity. It will at least be of service to me in that respect; it will teach me in future *not* to think everybody is in love with me.

'Yet I should like to have seen him before he went, for perhaps it may be many years before we meet again. By his manner of leaving us, however, he seems to have been perfectly indifferent about it. How very odd that he should go without giving us notice of it, or taking leave of anyone! But it is just like a young man, governed by the whim of the moment, or actuated merely by the love of doing anything odd! Unaccountable beings indeed! And young women are equally ridiculous! I shall soon begin to think, like my aunt, that everything is going to sixes and sevens, and that the whole race of mankind are degenerating.'

She was just dressed, and on the point of leaving her room to make her personal enquires after Mrs Percival, when Miss Stanley knocked at her door, and on her being admitted, began in her usual strain a long harangue upon her father's being so shocking as to make Edward go at all, and upon Edward's being so horrid as to leave them at such an hour in the morning.

'You have no idea,' said she, 'how surprised I was when he came into my room to bid me goodbye –'

'Have you seen him then, this morning?' said Kitty.

'Oh yes! And I was so sleepy that I could not open my eyes. And so he said, "Camilla, goodbye to you, for I am going away. I have not time to take leave of anybody else, and I dare not trust myself to see Kitty, for then you know I should never get away –"'

'Nonsense,' said Kitty; 'he did not say that, or he was in joke if he did.'

'Oh! no, I assure you he was as much in earnest as he ever was in his life; he was too much out of spirits to joke then. And he desired me, when we all met at breakfast, to give his compliments to your aunt, and his love to you, for you was a nice girl, he said, and he only wished it were in his power to be more with you. You were just the girl to suit him, because you were so lively and good-natured, and he wished with all his heart that you might not be married before he came back, for there was nothing he liked better than being here. Oh! You have no idea what fine things he said about you, till at last I fell asleep and he went away. But he certainly is in love with you – I am sure he is – I have thought so a great while, I assure you.'

'How can you be so ridiculous?' said Kitty, smiling with pleasure; 'I do not believe him to be so easily affected. But he did desire his love to me then? And wished I might not be married before his return? And said I was a nice girl, did he?'

'Oh! dear, yes, and I assure you it is the greatest praise in his opinion that he can bestow on anybody; I can hardly ever persuade him to call *me* one, though I beg him sometimes for an hour together.'

'And do you really think that he was sorry to go.'

'Oh! you can have no idea how wretched it made him. He would not have gone this month if my father had not insisted on it; Edward told me so himself yesterday. He said that he wished with all his heart he had never promised to go abroad, for that he repented it more and more every day; that it interfered with all his other schemes, and that since Papa had spoken to him about it, he was more unwilling to leave Chetwynde than ever.'

'Did he really say all this? And why would your father insist upon his going? – "His leaving England interfered with all his other plans, and his conversation with Mr Stanley had made him still more averse to it." – What can this mean!'

'Why, that he is excessively in love with you to be sure; what other plans can he have? And I suppose my father said that if he had not been going abroad, he should have wished him to marry you immediately. But I must go and see your aunt's plants. There is one of them that I quite dote on – and two or three more besides –'

'Can Camilla's explanation be true?' said Catharine to herself, when her friend had left the room. 'And after all my doubts and uncertainties, can Stanley really be averse to leaving England for *my sake* only? – His plans interrupted – and what indeed can his plans be, but towards marriage. Yet *so soon* to be in love with me! – But it is the effect perhaps only of the warmth of heart which to *me* is the highest recommendation in anyone. A heart disposed to love – and such under the appearance of so much gaiety and inattention – is Stanley's. Oh! how much does it endear him to me! But he is gone – gone perhaps for years – obliged to tear himself from what he most loves, his happiness is sacrificed to the vanity of his father! In what anguish he must have left the house! Unable to see me, or to bid me adieu, while I, senseless wretch, was daring to sleep. This, then, explained his leaving us at such a time of day. He could not trust himself to see me. Charming young man! How much must you have suffered! I *knew* that it was impossible for one so elegant and so well bred to leave any family in such a manner, but for a motive like this unanswerable.' Satisfied beyond the power of change of this, she went in high spirits to her aunt's apartment, without giving a moment's recollection on the vanity of young women, or the unaccountable conduct of young men.

Kitty continued in this state of satisfaction during the remainder of the Stanleys' visit, who took their leave with many pressing invitations to visit them in London, when, as Camilla said, she might have an opportunity of becoming acquainted with that sweet girl Augusta Halifax – or rather, thought Kitty, of seeing my dear Mary Wynne again. Mrs Percival, in answer to Mrs Stanley's invitation, replied that she looked upon London as the hothouse of vice where virtue had long been banished from society, and wickedness of every description was daily gaining ground; that Kitty was of herself sufficiently inclined to give way to, and indulge in vicious inclinations, and therefore was the last girl in the world to be trusted in London, as she would be totally unable to withstand temptation.

After the departure of the Stanleys Kitty returned to her usual occupations, but alas! they had lost their power of pleasing. Her bower alone retained its interest in her feelings, and perhaps that was owing to the particular remembrance it brought to her mind of Edward Stanley.

The summer passed away unmarked by any incident worth narrating, or any pleasure to Catharine save one, which arose from the receipt of a letter from her friend Cecilia, now Mrs Lascelles, announcing the speedy return of herself and husband to England.

A correspondence productive indeed of little pleasure to either party had been established between Camilla and Catharine. The latter had now lost the only satisfaction she had ever received from the letters of Miss Stanley, as that young lady, having informed her friend of the departure of her brother to Lyons, now never mentioned his name – her letters seldom contained any intelligence except a description of some new article of dress, an enumeration of various engagements, a panegyric on Augusta Halifax, and perhaps a little abuse of the unfortunate Sir Peter.

The Grove, for so was the mansion of Mrs Percival at Chetwynde denominated, was situated within five miles from Exeter, but though that lady possessed a carriage and horses of her own, it was seldom that Catharine could prevail on her to visit that town for the purpose of shopping, on account of the many officers perpetually quartered there and who infested the principal streets.

A company of strolling players on their way from some neighbouring races having opened a temporary theatre there, Mrs Percival was prevailed on by her niece to indulge her by attending the performance once during their stay. Mrs Percival insisted on paying Miss Dudley the compliment of inviting her to join the party, when a new difficulty arose, from the necessity of having some gentleman to attend them.

NOTES

LESLEY CASTLE

1. Henry Thomas Austen (1771–1850) was Jane Austen's favourite brother.

2. An early name for Brighton.

3. Vauxhall Gardens was a popular society venue in the eighteenth century, frequented both for its concerts and entertainment, and for its luxurious food.

4. An eighteenth-century French song which became popular throughout Europe.

5. Although the first three are expressions of praise ('good', 'excellent', 'again'), the remainder are simply musical instructions from the score ('from the beginning', 'moderately fast', 'with feeling' and 'a little faster').

6. In order for a marriage to be annulled in the Catholic Church, the Pope had to issue a Bull of Dispensation.

THE HISTORY OF ENGLAND

1. A parody of Oliver Goldsmith's *The History of England in a Series of Letters from a Nobleman to his Son* (1764).

2. Jane Austen imbues her 'partial, prejudiced, and ignorant historian' with her own pro-Stuart views.

3. Cassandra Elizabeth Austen (1773–1845), Jane Austen's only sister and the illustrator of this work.

4. The Revd George Austen (1731–1805), Jane Austen's father and the rector of Steventon and Deane in Hampshire.

5. Goldsmith's *History of England* was lambasted for the paucity of its dates.

6. Sir William Gascoigne (*c.*1350–1419), Chief Justice of the King's Bench.

7. Lord Cobham (Sir John Oldcastle, *c.*1378–1417), a former friend of Henry V and the inspiration for Shakespeare's Falstaff.

8. Nicholas Rowe's *The Tragedy of Jane Shore: Written in Imitation of Shakespeare's Style* (1714).

9. See, in particular *The History of King Richard III* (1557) by Sir Thomas More (1478–1535).

10. Perkin Warbeck (*c.*1474–99) and Lambert Simnel (*c.*1477–*c.*1534) were both pretenders to the throne during the reign of Henry VII; Perkin Warbeck initially claimed to be Edward, Earl of Warwick (as Lambert Simnel had claimed before him), and then to be Richard, Duke of York, younger brother of Edward V.

11. Here begins the narrator's unashamed eulogising of Mary Queen of Scots.

12. Words attributed to Wolsey in Goldsmith's *History of England*.

13. One of the few dates given in Goldsmith's *History of England*.

14. Delamere was the hero of *Emmeline, The Orphan of the Castle* (1788) by Charlotte Smith (1749–1806); William Gilpin (1724–1804) was the author of *Observations on*

several parts of Great Britain, particularly the High-lands of Scotland, relative chiefly to picturesque beauty, made in the year 1776, a work frequently referred to by Jane Austen.

15. Mr Whitaker is believed to have been a neighbour of the Austens; Mrs Lefroy was married to the rector of the neighbouring parish; Mrs Knight was connected to the Austens by marriage.

16. Jane Austen is referring to her brother, Francis William Austen (1774–1865), at that time a midshipman on board the *Perseverance*. He went on to become Admiral of the Fleet.

17. A reference to the Gunpowder Plot of 1605; it was by means of a letter to Lord Mounteagle, warning him to stay away, that the plot was uncovered.

18. Sheridan's *The Critic, or a Tragedy Rehearsed* (1779).

CATHARINE, OR THE BOWER

1. See note 3 to 'The History of England'.

2. 'The Beautiful Cassandra' was another of Austen's juvenilia, written in twelve chapters, of which the longest was only four sentences.

3. Charlotte Smith (1749–1806) was a popular Gothic novelist; *Emmeline, The Orphan of the Castle* (1788) was her first novel, followed by *Ethelinde* in 1790.

4. Ranelagh gardens became popular as a place to escape the city and take in the cleaner air in Chelsea. Balls, concerts, dinners and of course gossip were shared here almost daily.

5. Here probably 'difficult to please' or 'critical'.

6. William Pitt (1759–1806) was Prime Minister in 1792, when 'Catharine' was written; the Lord Chancellor was Edward Thurlow (1731–1806).

7. Four volumes of *Sermons* by Hugh Blair (1718–1800) were published between 1777 and 1794, with the final volume appearing posthumously in 1801; *Coelebs in Search of a Wife* by Hannah More (1745–1833), which exposed the corruption within the Regency, appeared in 1809. This was added in by Jane Austen at a later date, replacing her original reference: Secker's *Lectures on the Catechism of the Church of England* (1769). All three works were immensely popular in their time.

BIOGRAPHICAL NOTE

Jane Austen was born in 1775 in Steventon, Hampshire, the seventh of eight children. Her father, the Revd George Austen, was a well-read and cultured man, and Jane was mostly educated at home. She read voraciously as a child, in particular the works of Fielding, Sterne, Richardson and Scott. She also began writing at a very young age, producing *Love and Friendship* when she was only fourteen. *The History of England* followed when she was sixteen, and *A Collection of Letters* at seventeen.

Following her father's death in 1805, she and her mother moved to Southampton, before settling in Chawton, Hampshire, in 1809, and it was here that her major novels were written. Despite leading a remarkably uneventful life herself – she never married and seldom left home – her works are noted for their incredible powers of observation. Only four novels were published during her lifetime – *Sense and Sensibility* (1811), *Pride and Prejudice* (1813), *Mansfield Park* (1814) and *Emma* (1816) – and all were published anonymously. On a rare visit from home, she was taken ill and she died from Addison's disease in 1817. Two further novels, *Persuasion* and *Northanger Abbey*, were published posthumously in 1818. *Sanditon*, the novel she was working on when she died, appeared in 1925.

SELECTED TITLES FROM HESPERUS PRESS

Author	Title	Foreword writer
Edmondo de Amicis	*Constantinople*	Umberto Eco
Jane Austen	*Love and Friendship*	Fay Weldon
Honoré de Balzac	*Colonel Chabert*	A.N. Wilson
Charles Baudelaire	*On Wine and Hashish*	Margaret Drabble
Giovanni Boccaccio	*Life of Dante*	A.N. Wilson
Charlotte Brontë	*The Spell*	
Emily Brontë	*Poems of Solitude*	Helen Dunmore
Mikhail Bulgakov	*Fatal Eggs*	Doris Lessing
Mikhail Bulgakov	*The Heart of a Dog*	A.S. Byatt
Giacomo Casanova	*The Duel*	Tim Parks
Miguel de Cervantes	*The Dialogue of the Dogs*	Ben Okri
Geoffrey Chaucer	*The Parliament of Birds*	
Anton Chekhov	*The Story of a Nobody*	Louis de Bernières
Anton Chekhov	*Three Years*	William Fiennes
Wilkie Collins	*The Frozen Deep*	
Joseph Conrad	*Heart of Darkness*	A.N. Wilson
Joseph Conrad	*The Return*	Colm Tóibín
Gabriele D'Annunzio	*The Book of the Virgins*	Tim Parks
Dante Alighieri	*The Divine Comedy: Inferno*	
Dante Alighieri	*New Life*	Louis de Bernières
Daniel Defoe	*The King of Pirates*	Peter Ackroyd
Marquis de Sade	*Incest*	Janet Street-Porter
Charles Dickens	*The Haunted House*	Peter Ackroyd
Charles Dickens	*A House to Let*	
Fyodor Dostoevsky	*The Double*	Jeremy Dyson
Fyodor Dostoevsky	*Poor People*	Charlotte Hobson
Alexandre Dumas	*One Thousand and One Ghosts*	
George Eliot	*Amos Barton*	Matthew Sweet
Henry Fielding	*Jonathan Wild the Great*	Peter Ackroyd

F. Scott Fitzgerald	*The Popular Girl*	Helen Dunmore
Gustave Flaubert	*Memoirs of a Madman*	Germaine Greer
Ugo Foscolo	*Last Letters of Jacopo Ortis*	Valerio Massimo Manfredi
Elizabeth Gaskell	*Lois the Witch*	Jenny Uglow
Théophile Gautier	*The Jinx*	Gilbert Adair
André Gide	*Theseus*	
Johann Wolfgang von Goethe	*The Man of Fifty*	A.S. Byatt
Nikolai Gogol	*The Squabble*	Patrick McCabe
E.T.A. Hoffmann	*Mademoiselle de Scudéri*	Gilbert Adair
Victor Hugo	*The Last Day of a Condemned Man*	Libby Purves
Aldous Huxley	*After the Fireworks*	Fay Weldon
Joris-Karl Huysmans	*With the Flow*	Simon Callow
Henry James	*In the Cage*	Libby Purves
Franz Kafka	*Metamorphosis*	Martin Jarvis
Franz Kafka	*The Trial*	Zadie Smith
John Keats	*Fugitive Poems*	Andrew Motion
Heinrich von Kleist	*The Marquise of O–*	Andrew Miller
Mikhail Lermontov	*A Hero of Our Time*	Doris Lessing
Nikolai Leskov	*Lady Macbeth of Mtsensk*	Gilbert Adair
Carlo Levi	*Words are Stones*	Anita Desai
Xavier de Maistre	*A Journey Around my Room*	Alain de Botton
André Malraux	*The Way of the Kings*	Rachel Seiffert
Katherine Mansfield	*Prelude*	William Boyd
Edgar Lee Masters	*Spoon River Anthology*	Shena Mackay
Guy de Maupassant	*Butterball*	Germaine Greer
Prosper Mérimée	*Carmen*	Philip Pullman
Sir Thomas More	*The History of King Richard III*	Sister Wendy Beckett
Sándor Pëtofi	*John the Valiant*	George Szirtes
Francis Petrarch	*My Secret Book*	Germaine Greer

Luigi Pirandello	*Loveless Love*	
Edgar Allan Poe	*Eureka*	Sir Patrick Moore
Alexander Pope	*The Rape of the Lock* and *A Key to the Lock*	Peter Ackroyd
Antoine-François Prévost	*Manon Lescaut*	Germaine Greer
Marcel Proust	*Pleasures and Days*	A.N. Wilson
Alexander Pushkin	*Dubrovsky*	Patrick Neate
Alexander Pushkin	*Ruslan and Lyudmila*	Colm Tóibín
François Rabelais	*Pantagruel*	Paul Bailey
François Rabelais	*Gargantua*	Paul Bailey
Christina Rossetti	*Commonplace*	Andrew Motion
George Sand	*The Devil's Pool*	Victoria Glendinning
Jean-Paul Sartre	*The Wall*	Justin Cartwright
Friedrich von Schiller	*The Ghost-seer*	Martin Jarvis
Mary Shelley	*Transformation*	
Percy Bysshe Shelley	*Zastrozzi*	Germaine Greer
Stendhal	*Memoirs of an Egotist*	Doris Lessing
Robert Louis Stevenson	*Dr Jekyll and Mr Hyde*	Helen Dunmore
Theodor Storm	*The Lake of the Bees*	Alan Sillitoe
Leo Tolstoy	*The Death of Ivan Ilych*	
Leo Tolstoy	*Hadji Murat*	Colm Tóibín
Ivan Turgenev	*Faust*	Simon Callow
Mark Twain	*The Diary of Adam and Eve*	John Updike
Mark Twain	*Tom Sawyer, Detective*	
Oscar Wilde	*The Portrait of Mr W.H.*	Peter Ackroyd
Virginia Woolf	*Carlyle's House and Other Sketches*	Doris Lessing
Virginia Woolf	*Monday or Tuesday*	Scarlett Thomas
Emile Zola	*For a Night of Love*	A.N. Wilson